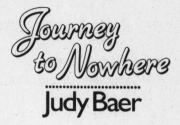

Journey
to Nowhere

Judy Baer

Cedar River Daydreams

Other Books by Judy Baer

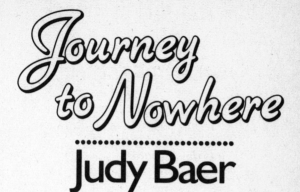

Journey to Nowhere

Judy Baer

BETHANY HOUSE PUBLISHERS
MINNEAPOLIS, MINNESOTA 55438
A Division of Bethany Fellowship, Inc.

Journey to Nowhere
Judy Baer

Library of Congress Catalog Card Number 88–63462

ISBN 1-55661-067-X

Published by Bethany House Publishers
A Division of Bethany Fellowship, Inc.
6820 Auto Club Road, Minneapolis, Minnesota 55438

Printed in the United States of America

For Ann Z.

JUDY BAER received a B.A. in English and Education from Concordia College in Moorhead, Minnesota. She has had twelve novels published and is a member of the National Romance Writers of America, the Society of Children's Book Writers and the National Federation of Press Women.

Two of her novels have been prizewinning best-sellers in the Bethany House SPRINGFLOWER SERIES (for girls 12–15); *Adrienne* and *Paige*. Both books have been awarded first place for juvenile fiction in the National Federation of Press Women's communications contest.

Chapter One

"Good job, Jennifer. Well done." There was a note of admiration in Mrs. Drummond's voice as she handed Jennifer Golden her test paper.

Lexi Leighton looked up from her own newly graded paper to glance at Jennifer who was gazing happily down at the folder in her hand. Jennifer's eyes were wide with delight, and an impish grin played at the corners of her lips.

"The assignment for tomorrow is on the board. I'd advise reading it very carefully. You *never know* when there's going to be a quiz on the material."

A chorus of groans resounded.

Mrs. Drummond only smiled, tucked her red pencil into the wave of blond hair over her ear, turned and began erasing the blackboard. Lexi smacked her own book shut with an energetic snap and hurried to catch up with Jennifer, who was already on her way out the classroom door.

" 'Good job, Jennifer. Well done,' " Lexi imitated. "Awright!" They slapped hands gleefully and Lexi's dark eyes danced with pleasure. The two girls made a pretty picture standing together in the long hallway—a tall blond with Scandinavian blue eyes and a shorter brown-haired beauty with eyes the color of rich chocolate.

"Not so bad for a former dunce, huh?" Jennifer couldn't suppress her grin.

Lexi gave her a prod in the ribs. "You were never a dunce. You know that."

Jennifer shrugged. "Maybe. But that's the way I felt."

What a change! Lexi thought to herself. A complete turnabout from the sullen, unhappy girl Jennifer had been only weeks ago. "I'm proud of you, Jenna," she murmured softly. "Really. What you're doing can't be easy."

Jennifer shrugged nonchalantly. "What I'm doing now is a whole lot easier than what I've had to do my entire life, Lexi. At least now when I get mixed up or make a muddle of something, the teachers don't act disgusted." She brightened. "For once, they understand!" Jennifer glanced at her wristwatch. "Of course, they *still* don't understand being late for class. . . ."

"See you at noon?" Lexi asked.

"Of course," Jennifer replied as she turned down the hallway to her next class.

Lexi wandered at a more leisurely pace toward the school office to pick up a camera. She had a pass from Mrs. Drummond to leave study hall so she could take some pictures for the school paper. Now was as good a time as any to get started.

As she walked, her mind drifted to Jennifer—or, rather, the new person that Jennifer had become.

What a difference a single word could make!

Dyslexia. A learning disability.

Before that diagnosis Jennifer had considered herself stupid because she was unable to read or complete homework without great difficulty. Even the teachers had labeled her rebellious because she was so obviously bright and yet not keeping up in class. Now that her problem had a name, people had begun to realize that Jennifer's dyslexia was at the heart of her school problems—not uncooperativeness or rebellion. Already Jennifer's self-esteem had begun to return.

"Whatcha thinking about?" came the soft question near Lexi's ear.

She smiled. There was no need to turn her head. The low male voice and the faint scent of cologne told Lexi all she needed to know.

"Hi, Todd." She smiled into his dark blue eyes.

"Hi, yourself. Why so deep in thought?" He fell in step beside her, his muscular arm brushing against her slender one.

"I've been thinking about Jennifer."

"Quite a change, I'd say." When he smiled, a tiny, hesitant dimple winked in his cheek.

"She's like a different person ever since they told her she had a learning disability."

"It couldn't have hurt either to hear that her IQ"—he gestured his thumb upward—"is right up there."

"It's funny, isn't it?" Lexi murmured as they walked to class. "She thought she was dumb and she's got one of the highest IQ's in the school!"

"Now that everyone knows what her problem is at least they can work with it," Todd concluded cheerfully. "But I didn't catch up with you so that we could discuss Jennifer."

"Why then?" Lexi teased. "Is this a business visit?"

"Sort of. Are you going to take those pictures of the new band uniforms today?"

"I'm on my way to pick up a camera. If there's no one in the band room to put on a uniform for me, I'll need a model. Care to volunteer?"

"Nah. I'll take the picture and *you* wear the uniform. Less stress on the camera."

They walked companionably toward the administrative offices. Todd was chief photographer of the *Review* and Lexi his chief assistant. Between them, they managed to keep a visual tab on the happenings of Cedar River High School—and each other.

The administrative offices were surrounded by walls of glass. Lexi could see a secretary typing furiously and two red lights flashing on a bank of telephones. Lexi's camera was already on the work table near the paper cutter.

"I see Mrs. McMartin has already put out the camera. I'll just go in and—" She stopped as Todd let out a long, low whistle.

"Trouble again."

She turned to stare at him. "Where? I don't see any—" Then her gaze fell on the row of chairs outside the principal's office. "Oh."

The string of steel chairs lining one wall of the office was empty except for a solitary figure slouched low in one seat. Looking defiant, his dark head resting against the wall, his feet stretching out before him, he sat with his hands shoved deep into his pockets.

"Matt's in trouble again."

"You mean *still*," Lexi corrected. "Matt's in trouble *still*."

Todd grimaced. "Yeah, now that Jennifer's been straightened out, he's left to carry the whole load for causing an uproar."

"Speaking of Jennifer, I wonder if she's still seeing him," Lexi mused. "She doesn't say much about it, but I know they are friends. Matt was the one person she seemed comfortable with when she was having all her trouble in school." Lexi's brow furrowed. "I suppose when you feel like rebelling, you have to make friends with rebels. I wonder why she doesn't mention him now."

"She probably doesn't dare. You know Matt's reputation."

"Still, when she was having so many problems, the two seemed to get along."

Todd grinned wickedly. "Yeah, when Minda Hannaford wasn't getting in the way."

Minda *did* have a habit of getting in the way—especially when someone else had her eye on a boy Minda was interested in getting to know. Before Lexi could respond, Todd slipped into the office and retrieved the camera. Matt never even glanced upward to see who had walked past him.

————

At noon the cafeteria was a constant hum of noise as everyone got caught up on the latest happenings.

Jennifer was already at "their" table with Binky McNaughton and Peggy Madison when Lexi wound her way through the maze of tables to meet them.

"Where were you?" Binky questioned. "We're planning a party." She was skinny and birdlike, with shoulder-length hair woven into a French braid that seemed to be coming undone. A halo of reddish-brown strands framed Binky's face. Lexi felt as though she were being scolded by a little house wren.

"Without me?" Lexi emptied her tray and sat down. She tried to ignore the painted block walls of the cafeteria and the drab gray tables and benches. "What are we doing?"

"Peggy's house."

"Tonight."

"At nine o'clock."

"Bring tapes."

"And a sleeping bag."

"With a pillow."

Lexi stirred at her beef stew, listening to the staccato instructions. "Sounds good to me."

"What sounds good?" Todd plopped into the seat beside her. Egg McNaughton, a tall, gangly version of Binky, loomed over them.

"We're staying at Peggy's tonight, that's all."

"Good!" Egg interjected. "I hate it when you stay at our place. I never get any sleep."

"That's because you stay up half the night with your ear to our door trying to hear what we're saying," Jennifer pointed out with cheerful maliciousness.

"Do not."

"Do too."

"Do not."

"Who was it who fell into the room at three A.M. when I opened the door to go to the bathroom?" Binky asked sweetly, batting her pale eyelashes in her brother's direction.

Todd gave his friend an incredulous stare. "You did that, Egg? Really?" Todd made a valiant effort not to laugh out loud.

Poor Egg couldn't speak. His face had turned the color of the cherry Jell-O on his plate and he seemed to have something stuck in his throat.

Todd slapped his hand against his thigh and began to laugh.

"It's not funny," Egg managed to squeak, his very obvious adam's apple bobbing in his throat. "They were talking about *us*."

Todd's eyebrows arched upward. "What did they say?" Lexi could see he was hard pressed to keep from laughing.

Egg dropped his chin toward his chest. His long neck seemed to fold in half. "I don't know. I think Binky stuck something in the keyhole."

"An ear plug," she announced. "The squishy pink kind I use for swimming. Works great for keeping nosey brothers in their place."

Jennifer snorted and covered her mouth with her hand. Egg's neck reddened even more.

"Well, *I* don't have any brothers to bother us," Peggy pointed out. "So we won't have any problems like that tonight!" Then she glanced at her watch. "Gotta go. See you all later."

When Peggy had left, Egg sat down in her place. "I'll bet she's going to meet Chad." When he said "Chad" he crossed his hands over his heart and pasted a lovesick expression on his features.

"Don't press it, Egg," his sister warned. "You get pretty silly yourself sometimes over members of the opposite sex." She paused for effect. "Like Minda Hannaford."

Egg's face shut down immediately and Lexi felt a pang of sympathy for the gangly boy. At least Peggy and Chad had a relationship. Minda still didn't seem to know that Egg existed.

"These girls are pretty tough today, Egg, old boy," Todd observed matter-of-factly. "Come on, I'm going to go and talk to the coach. You'd better come too. I think you'll be safer with me."

One by one they abandoned the table until only Lexi and Binky were left. "Going straight home after school?" Binky wondered.

Lexi nodded. "My little brother Ben will be waiting. He wants me to 'report in' so he can tell me everything that happened at the academy." Ben Leighton attended an academy for handicapped children and insisted that each night Lexi listen to his recitation of the day's activities.

"Me too. I have to do some chores for my mom. Meet you at the west door after school." Binky, suddenly in a hurry, didn't wait for Lexi's answer.

————

After school, Binky was already waiting when Lexi arrived. The stack of books in her arm weighed down her entire left side.

"Planning to study this weekend, or are you going to pump iron?" Lexi eyed the huge stack of books that Binky clutched. "I think they weigh more than you do."

"It seems every one of my teachers thought it would be a great idea to have a test on Monday!" Binky wailed. "It's not fair! How do teachers know when you have something planned? They must. They manage to ruin it every time."

"You can study Saturday," Lexi soothed.

"Yeah, but it's ruining a perfectly good weekend . . ." Binky's voice trailed away.

Lexi glanced at her tiny friend. "Bink? What's wrong."

"Look."

Lexi's gaze followed the same path that Binky's had taken. Across the school yard and on the far side of the street stood Matt Windsor.

It seemed to Lexi that Matt never stood upright. Today he lounged against the fender of a big navy car, his legs crossed at the ankles, the sharp points of his boots glinting wickedly. His arms were wrapped across his chest in a wary, protective gesture, and his black hair gleamed in the sunlight.

It occurred to Lexi that Matt could have stepped off a movie screen portraying some boy-gone-wrong. She studied him thoughtfully. Or, maybe that's exactly who Matt was—a boy gone wrong.

Her imagination was running away with her again, Lexi told herself. She'd read too many mysteries lately. Vowing to stick to safer reading material like history and the backs of cereal boxes, Lexi turned away from the sight of Matt.

Long after she and Binky had parted, and even after supper as she made her way to Peggy's house at the end of the street, a sense of foreboding remained with Lexi.

There was something wrong with Matt. The bad feeling she had about him would not go away.

Matt Windsor was dangerous. It was obvious he was dangerous to himself, but was he also dangerous to other people?

Chapter Two

"Are you absolutely certain your mother doesn't mind?" Binky asked, a worried expression and a blotch of chocolate marking her brow. "We're making a pretty big mess."

"Nah. She said we could bake." Peggy dipped unconcernedly into a mixing bowl and retrieved a glossy lump of chocolate batter. She opened her mouth wide and plopped it onto her tongue.

"Is the popcorn ready yet, Lexi?" Jennifer wondered. "I think I've melted enough butter to grease a car."

"Ready." Lexi carried a massive bowl of white kernels to the table. "Shouldn't the pizza be here by now?"

"I just saw the delivery truck pull up in the driveway. Who has money?" Peggy dashed for the front door.

By the time the four girls carried all their food from the kitchen to Peggy's bedroom, a third of it had already disappeared. Peggy dashed downstairs to find another liter of pop while her friends lounged on the bedroom floor eating and talking.

"Popcorn is my absolute favorite food," Jennifer announced to no one in particular. She lay on her back, her blond hair haloing her head, popping one kernel at a time into her mouth.

"No, chocolate!" Binky protested. "Any kind— milk chocolate, semisweet chocolate, fudge, chocolate chips, chocolate milk, chocolate bunnies, Cocoa Puffs, chocolate cake, chocolate pie—"

"Don't you people know anything about nutrition?" Lexi asked. "Now, pizza, *there's* a nutritious food! All the basic food groups. The pepperoni is meat, the crust is bread, the mushrooms are vegetables, the cheese is milk—"

"A chocolate pizza might be nice," Binky sighed.

"Better yet, a chocolate popcorn pizza!" Jennifer added with a giggle.

"Yuk!" Peggy wrinkled her face as she returned to the room holding two liters of soda. "Gross! What are you talking about?"

"Never mind," Lexi chuckled. "I think I'm getting full."

"Me too." Jennifer eyed the empty containers. "And sick."

"Don't get sick!" Binky yelped. "Do something so that you don't think about your stomach."

"Like what?"

"I don't know. Talk."

"About what?" Jennifer was holding her stomach and rocking back and forth. She looked a little green.

"Food?" Peggy offered unhelpfully.

Jennifer groaned.

"School?"

Jennifer groaned again.

"Wait a minute," Lexi pointed out. "You don't

need to groan about school anymore. You're doing great."

"Better, at least," Jennifer acknowledged. "I can use my books on tape without being worried anyone will see me. Even the teachers help me find material that is recorded on cassette. What a time saver."

"That, and your new computer."

Jennifer brightened and the green seemed to fade from her complexion. "It's great. Even though I still mix things up on the computer, at least it looks better! Now I don't get comments anymore about my terrible writing."

Lexi remained quiet. She'd had no idea how devastating a learning disability could be, but she was realizing more every day what Jennifer had gone through.

Jennifer looked thoughtful. "I guess the best thing is the relief I feel at knowing what's wrong with me."

The four girls were silent for a long, thoughtful moment. Then Jennifer clutched her middle and groaned again.

"Boys!" Binky squealed. "Let's talk about boys! That gets your mind off anything!"

Lexi burst out laughing at Binky's intense announcement. Poor Binky. She was so tiny and young looking, she hardly seemed ready to be out of grade school. That was tough, considering it was the beginning of her sophomore year of high school.

"What boys did you have in mind, Bink?" Lexi teased. "Anyone special?"

Binky looked disgusted. "No. I wish there were."

"I know what you mean," Peggy murmured. "I'm glad I have someone special now."

Lexi studied her friend for a long moment and a sense of regret passed through her. It had been more fun before Peggy and Chad started seeing so much of each other. She'd hardly mentioned him over the summer but lately . . . Lexi stirred at the popcorn. She, Todd, Binky, Egg and Jennifer were still the same—good friends. Romance would be nice, but Lexi knew her parents frowned on kids her age getting serious about anyone. Besides, they had too much fun to try to rock the boat.

Seeing the dreamy look in Peggy's eyes, Jennifer promptly made a show of pretending to stick her finger in her mouth. She made some wretched gagging sounds. "Peggy's in love."

Peggy blinked and gathered her wits about her enough to shoot back. "What about you? You were hanging around with Matt Windsor!"

Jennifer sat up cross-legged and put her elbows on her knees. "But I started hanging around with him for all the wrong reasons."

"What do you mean?" Binky wondered, busy taking it all in.

"Because I thought Matt was bad. I wanted to get the attention away from the trouble I was having in school and thought hooking up with him would be a sure-fire way to do it."

"You were right on that account," Peggy agreed. She shivered. "Matt scares me. He looks so . . . wild."

"He's not so bad," Jennifer defended. "He was always nice to me."

"Todd told me once that Matt used to be different," Lexi interjected, "and that the change occurred about three years ago."

Jennifer nodded thoughtfully. "I guess that's

true. I really didn't know Matt then, but I don't remember any black leather jacket—"

"—or cigarettes—"

"—or locker full of tardy slips . . ."

Jennifer frowned. "You don't know Matt. Don't
be in such a big hurry to decide what he's like."

"You're *defending* him?" Peggy sounded surprised. "He's a hood, Jennifer."

"Maybe."

"*For sure.*"

"You can't say that. Not really." Jennifer paused
to choose her words carefully. "When I got my hair
cut and started running around with him, I didn't
feel like a hood."

"How *did* you feel?" Lexi asked softly. "Can you
tell us?"

Jennifer unfolded and stood up. "Hurt, angry,
mad, confused. I never felt mean—even if I acted that
way." She paced back and forth across the small bedroom. "Maybe that's how Matt feels."

"Who'd know? He never talks to anyone—except
you."

"And Minda," Binky added. "The way she's been
chasing him he can't help it. He trips over her every
time he moves."

"Doesn't it make you curious about him?" Lexi
said, her voice low. "Do you ever wonder why—"

"Why what?"

"Why he dresses and acts the ways he does."

"That's just like you, Lexi, to try to figure out
what's going on inside somebody else's head." Peggy
sounded irritated. "Maybe he doesn't have reasons
for what he does. Maybe he's just wild . . . and scary
. . . and mean."

Lexi didn't accept that for a minute, and she could see that Jennifer didn't either. She let the subject drop until Binky and Peggy got involved in doing each other's hair. Then, quietly, she slipped to Jennifer's side.

"You're worried, aren't you?"

Jennifer looked up, startled. "About what?"

"Matt."

Jennifer sighed. "Kind of. I don't know him very well, but he isn't as bad as everyone seems to think." She stared out the window into the darkness. "Sometimes I wish . . ." and her voice trailed away.

"Wished what, Jenna?"

She shrugged. "It's just that I still remember how rotten it was to think of myself as dumb and not able to keep up. Now that I'm finally feeling good about myself, it makes me wish that Matt could too."

"What makes you think he feels bad?" Lexi studied Jennifer's face intently.

"He never smiles. Not really. Oh, sometimes his lips move but his eyes never change. They're always flat and black like stones that don't reflect any light." Jennifer gave Lexi an anguished look. "It's hard to explain, but I know he's not happy. I just *know* it."

It was then that Peggy and Binky descended upon them to experiment with two new hairstyles they'd discovered in the magazines on Peggy's bed.

Nothing more was said about Matt Windsor, though his presence seemed to hover between Lexi and Jennifer.

Chapter Three

"I think I ate too much this weekend," Jennifer complained as she and Lexi exchanged books in their lockers between classes. "It feels like a bowling ball is stuck in my stomach."

Before Lexi could respond, Minda Hannaford stuck her pale blond head between the two girls. "*Looks* like a bowling ball too."

"Thank you, Minda, for that bit of helpful information!" Jennifer shot back.

"Just pointing out the *obvious*." Minda's blue eyes fluttered and she smiled so sweetly that anyone watching at a distance would have thought she was paying Jennifer the world's nicest compliment.

"What's obvious, Minda, is that you got out on the wrong side of the bed. Why don't you go home and start the day over?"

"Because I've got plans, that's why."

Jennifer glared with contempt. "Pity the poor person you have them with."

Minda looked sly and Lexi immediately realized that this was the reason Minda had started the conversation at all. She had information to impart.

"Matt, you mean? I doubt he's feeling sorry for himself."

Jennifer darted Lexi a quick, understanding look. "So that's what this is all about, Minda. You wanted me to know that you and Matt have plans. Is that it?"

"Does it bother you?" The tone in Minda's voice indicated she hoped fervently that it did.

"Not a bit. It's a free country. Matt can go slumming any time he likes."

That set even Minda aback. She was silent for a moment, trying to regroup, while Lexi pulled at Jennifer's arm. All she needed was for Jennifer and Minda to have a fistfight in the hallway. Spunky friends were one thing, but this bordered on the ridiculous.

"Come on, Jennifer," Lexi whispered. "Don't get started. She's trying to make you jealous."

"I can't be jealous. Matt and I are only friends."

"She doesn't know that. Anyway, for Minda, *everyone* is competition. Come on."

Lexi was saved from attempting to spirit Jennifer away by a commotion at the end of the hall.

Loud voices and the sound of scuffling turned all three girls' attention toward the small crowd that was beginning to gather.

"What's going on?" Minda wondered as she caught up with Lexi and Jennifer. "A fight?" She balanced on her tiptoes to see the action.

"Let's go," Lexi murmured, tugging at Jennifer's sleeve.

"No way. I want to see what's going on."

Jennifer struck off down the hall with Minda in her wake. Lexi hesitated for a moment, but then her curiosity compelled her to follow.

The crowd was growing rapidly.

Lexi couldn't see over the tops of the tallest boys' heads, but she could hear the sickening sound of fist against flesh and the occasional shudder of a locker as a body flew into it.

Egg McNaughton was standing at the edge of the fray watching with avid interest. His long, thin body moved and swayed as he clenched and unclenched his fists while he watched.

"Egg-O! What's going on?" Jennifer squeezed her way up beside him. Lexi held back but Minda started to shove her way front and center.

"Somebody crossed Matt Windsor, I guess. Looks like Matt wants to make breakfast out of him."

Matt! Even Lexi, who despised fights, moved a little closer.

She certainly couldn't fault Matt for not picking on someone his own size. Matt, who was slim, muscular and not quite six feet tall, was pounding on one of Cedar River's starting football line-up. A trickle of blood was oozing down the corner of Matt's lip and one eye looked suspiciously bruised, as if the colors blue and purple were not far behind.

His opponent, however, looked worse. He had a bloody nose that created a river of red flowing into his mouth. He was spitting and swinging and spitting again. Lexi covered her eyes.

Her shoulders sagged with relief when she heard the principal shout. "Stop it!" Without another word, he and two other teachers separated the flailing boys. It took two full-grown men to hold Matt back.

"I'll get you yet, you—"

"That's enough. Both of you! To my office. Now!"

Discreetly the audience faded away as the three men marched the stumbling boys down the hall.

Jennifer gave a low whistle. "I wonder what that was about."

"Do you think he's all right?" Minda whispered in alarm.

Lexi and Jennifer turned to stare at Minda. "Eddie? Sure. He's as strong as a horse."

"Not Eddie! Matt. He got hit in the eye and—"

"You can be sure Matt started this, Minda. And I wouldn't worry about him. Matt's been in plenty of fights."

Minda turned an angry glare on Jennifer. "If this is all the concern you have for Matt, then you can just stay away from him! You're no friend of his! Not a real one, at least."

Jennifer gave a startled blink, but Minda had already taken off down the hall in the direction of the administration offices, no doubt to see what she could learn about Matt's fate.

"What in the world made her so sensitive?"

Lexi sighed. "Matt is Minda's boy-of-the-moment, that's all."

"Is it a club she belongs to? Like a book-of-the-month club?" Jennifer scuffed her toe on the tile floor. "Poor Matt."

Lexi looked at her friend in surprise. "Poor Matt? He just about pulverized the biggest guy on the football team!"

"I know. But that's just the way I feel about him. He's real tough and mean and . . . vulnerable."

That went together like sweet, gooey and non-caloric in Lexi's mind, but she remained silent. She didn't know Matt—and really didn't want to—but it wasn't her place to judge.

The hallway was still buzzing with conversation about the fight.

"Did you see what he did to Eddie? I didn't think Windsor was that strong."

"He's wiry, though. I heard he lifts weights."

"Maybe Eddie is lucky. Somebody told me that the last time Matt got into a fight, he cut somebody with a knife."

"No kidding?"

"Those boots of his could hold a switchblade easy."

"You think so?"

"Sure. Haven't you ever seen that TV show where this guy . . ."

Lexi tuned out the conversation and headed for class. The Matt Windsor legend was already growing by leaps and bounds. With every comment or speculation, Matt got bigger, meaner, tougher, and more dangerous. Yet Jennifer's first reaction had been to feel sorry for Matt. It was a strange contrast.

Matt Windsor was a puzzle, no doubt about that.

————

Todd and Lexi had finished their work on the photos for the next edition of the *Review* and cleared off their work table when Egg came shambling in, looking all elbows and knees. His bony wrists hung two inches beneath the cuffs of his shirt.

Lexi turned away so as to not let Egg see her smile. He was so funny and endearing—all gawky and clumsy and sweet. He fell heavily into the chair nearest Todd.

"Have you heard?"

Todd glanced up from the pile of papers he was straightening. "Heard what?"

"About Windsor."

"Matt? No. What's going on?"

Lexi edged a little closer, curious.

"He's been suspended—for fighting."

"How long?"

"Haven't heard. It's sure to be a week, though. He roughed up Eddie pretty badly."

"Eddie gets hurt worse than that in football practice," Todd snorted. "He's just been crying about his wounds to dig Matt in deeper."

"Maybe. I know he hates Matt and it's worse now that Matt beat him like that. Hard on Eddie's ego."

"Poor Eddie," Todd said sarcastically. "I wonder why you never hear 'poor Matt.' "

Lexi listened with interest. She and Todd hadn't had much opportunity to discuss the fight or its ramifications. Somehow she'd expected that he'd be on Eddie's side. When she heard him making an attempt to defend Matt, her curiosity was piqued.

"I heard they found a knife on Matt. Think it's true?"

Todd stuck his hand in his pocket and pulled out a little silver pocket knife. "Have you heard about the knife I carry? Does that make me a candidate for reform school?"

Egg gave Todd a disgusted look. "That's different."

"Why? It's a knife."

"Yeah, but with *you* it's different . . ."

A dry chuckle escaped Todd. "Right. Because I live in the right part of town, have parents who earn a good living, and I don't wear black leather."

" . . . and you haven't got a police record for shop-lifting or friends that probably make their living selling drugs." Egg looked defiant.

"True," Todd admitted. "Maybe I just can't forget the way Matt was in grade school. We used to hang around together a lot. That's why I can't believe he's in so much trouble now."

"What was he like?" Lexi asked. "Please, tell me." She propped her elbows on the tabletop, cupped her chin in her hands and waited expectantly.

Todd dropped onto the chair between her and Egg. He crossed his ankles and stretched his arms behind his head. "He was quiet, mostly. Sometimes I thought he was shy."

"Well, he's still that. Quiet, I mean."

"That's because he never opens a book," Egg volunteered. "Who can talk when he doesn't know what he's talking about?"

"And he was sensitive."

Egg snorted. "Sorry, but I don't buy that."

Todd gave him an irritated look. "He was. I'll never forget the day his puppy got run over by a car. He sat right there in the middle of the street holding that little brown and white spaniel and crying like his heart would break." Todd appeared pensive. "Finally, someone called the police. He had traffic stopped for half a block. They came and picked him up, dog and all, and carried him to the sidewalk. When they tried to pry his fingers off the dog, it took two grown men to do it."

"That's so sad!" tenderhearted Lexi blurted.

"Sounds weird to me," Egg persisted, unwilling to be convinced that Matt was anything but a convict-waiting-to-happen.

Todd nodded. "Yeah. I thought it was kind of over-reacting too, but my mom explained it that night."

"What did she say?"

"Well, I didn't know it because Matt and I had just met that year, but apparently his mother and dad had terrible marriage problems. One night she took Matt's little sister with her and left Matt behind. They moved to Canada, Mom thought."

"How awful!"

"Yeah. Mom figures that the dog getting run over was the last straw. Matt's mother gave him that dog." Lexi noticed even Egg's eyes looked a little damp. "I never figured he'd had such a tough life!"

"I suppose it's no excuse for getting into trouble," Todd commented. "Still, I know there's something nice in Matt—if he'd just let it come out."

When Lexi glanced up, she was surprised to see how defeated Egg looked. "What's wrong, Egg?"

"Oh, nothing, I guess. It's just not fair."

"What isn't?"

Egg's funny, sweet face contorted in frustration. "Oh, I thought it was going to be easy to hate Matt Windsor. After all, he's a hood. There's no reason in the world that Minda Hannaford should be so crazy about him, and now you tell me all this . . ." His voice trailed away and Lexi and Todd exchanged a knowing glance.

So that was what this was all about! Minda. No wonder Egg had come down so hard on Matt. He was probably hoping someone would come and spirit Matt away to reform school and leave Minda's attentions free for him—as if that were likely to happen.

"Egg, don't get so down about Minda and Matt. You know how fickle she is. If it weren't Matt, it would be someone else she'd be chasing."

"Yeah. Everyone in the entire world except for me."

"Don't you think you're exaggerating just a little?"

"Not much. On Minda's priority of dates the only ones lower are in nursing homes."

That outrageous comment caused both Todd and Lexi to break into a gale of laughter. Even Egg's lip quirked into a smile.

"You are the saddest excuse for an optimist I've ever seen," Todd teased. "Lexi and I are done here. Why don't we close up and go pump a little iron in the gym?" He turned to Lexi. "You don't mind if we do that, do you?"

"No. I think Egg could use a little cheering up."

"And maybe Minda likes muscles," Egg piped up. "If I start lifting now, I'll be in good shape by—"

His face fell as Todd and Lexi finished in chorus "—the time you get to the nursing home!"

———

Egg's cheering up lasted all of three minutes. Lexi accompanied Todd and Egg to their workout. As they turned the corner toward the gym, they saw Minda lugging a load of books toward the doorway.

"You planning to study all night?" Todd asked.

Minda barely had time to look up. "These are Matt's. I thought I'd surprise him and bring them over to his house. That way, he can study at home and not get behind."

Lexi could see Egg's face crumpling.

"I can't remember Matt ever worrying about being behind," Todd commented. "Are you sure that's the reason he asked for the books?"

"Oh, he didn't exactly *ask* for them. I'm just doing this as a little surprise." With that she pushed her way out the door.

"I'll bet," Todd muttered. "She's going to chase Matt until *he* catches her."

The whole situation left a bad taste in Lexi's mouth. Matt, Minda, Egg. What a triangle! What a mess.

Chapter Four

The sun was bright and warm on Lexi's back as she walked her bike through a quiet intersection. Impatiently she looked to the right and then the left. Could she be lost? Lexi was positive this was the direction her father had told her to go. Or had he meant for her to turn *right* on Willard Avenue? Lexi studied the note with her father's nearly illegible scrawl and then looked again at the row of uninspired houses.

Surely the Wyssickys didn't live here! Lexi had met Mrs. Wyssicky when she brought one of her three French poodles into Dr. Leighton's office for a checkup. Could anyone who dyed her poodle's fur to match her outfit be comfortable living in one of these simple tract houses?

Lexi studied the street. It was a pleasant neighborhood, if slightly dull. Every house seemed to have been built from the same blueprint. The only distinguishing features were their color and the variety of half-grown trees in the front yards. There were a number of small children playing outside and Lexi could hear the rackety *clack-clack-clack* of racing Hot Wheels.

She propped her bike up against a tree and bent down to tie a shoelace that had come undone. When she stood up, she saw a couple involved in deep conversation leave one of the houses to stand on the driveway.

Lexi squinted curiously. Strange, but the boy looked familiar. She studied the lean, muscular profile . . . Matt! It was Matt Windsor.

He wasn't wearing his trademark black leather. Instead, he was in snug-fitting acid washed jeans and a tight, body hugging black T-shirt. Lexi could tell by the sharp, energetic movement of his hands that he felt strongly about what he was saying.

The woman—or girl—Lexi couldn't tell for sure how old she was—was gesturing just as violently as Matt.

Lexi could almost imagine the angry words they were exchanging. Matt was roughly running his fingers through his dark hair while the lady was stamping her foot furiously. Though Lexi knew she shouldn't be watching, she was too fascinated to move.

Was this his sister? she wondered. They didn't look alike. The girl was blond and fair. Hadn't Todd said Matt's sister had gone to Canada with her mother? Though she wore very short, tight shorts and was barefoot, she seemed older than the girls at school. Lexi lost herself in speculation.

Then the argument seemed to escalate. Matt was yelling and pointing an angry finger toward the street. The woman shook her head vehemently. Suddenly, her arm shot out and she brought her open palm across Matt's cheek.

Lexi could see the shock on his features. She found herself holding her breath. Would he hit her back?

Matt's fist clenched into a tight ball at his side, and Lexi remembered what he'd done to Eddie in the school hallway. Amazingly, the woman slapped him again, this time with the back of her hand. Lexi watched in wonder as Matt flinched. Without another word or gesture, he turned away.

Suddenly Lexi felt very conspicuous. Here she was, standing on a street corner, watching what appeared to be a very personal, very angry argument.

"Dad's going to have to deliver this medication himself," she muttered to herself. "I'm getting out of here." With that, she swung onto the seat of her ten-speed and raced toward home.

She'd seen it with her own eyes. Matt Windsor had allowed someone to slap him—not once, but twice, and he'd walked away.

Who was the woman who had such power?

And who was the *real* Matt Windsor?

———

The odd scene was still vivid in Lexi's mind when she saw Matt Windsor in the hallway two days later. His suspension over, he was back in school.

His black leather jacket was back in place, as were the high, pointed boots and the sullen, "dare-to-cross-me" expression on his face. He looked more unapproachable, more forbidding than ever. Lexi wondered anew at the little scene she'd seen acted out.

"Matt! Matt! I've been looking all over for you!"

Lexi turned around to see Minda racing toward

Matt with the determination of a bull charging a red cape.

Matt's only signal that he'd even heard Minda was the slight lifting of one eyebrow.

"I wanted to find you before you left the school. Some of the Hi-Fives are having a little get-together tonight at my place and I'd *love* to have you come." The Hi-Five was a very snobbish social club at Cedar River High. Minda's voice was so syrupy and sweet that Lexi almost felt cavities forming as she listened.

"It's going to be *intimate* and *private* and—"

"Sorry. Busy."

"Oh." Minda's face fell. Lexi was reminded of a balloon deflating as she watched Minda work hard to retain her smile. "But couldn't you just—"

"Can't."

"Well, I suppose it must be important, but . . ." Minda's voice faded into a whine. Lexi knew how Minda hated to be turned down. And Matt hadn't even bothered to give her a reason for the rejection other than a curt "busy."

As Minda turned away, Jennifer came strolling nonchalantly toward them. Unaware of the little scene Lexi had just witnessed, Jennifer gave Matt a cheerful smile and called, "Matthew! Hiya. Is that your new Harley in the parking lot? What a machine! I was looking at my dad's cycle magazines last night and . . ."

Lexi was rooted to the spot, transfixed by the little scene before her, even though she knew she had to be in class in less than three minutes.

Matt, who'd looked nothing but bored with Minda's flirtations, brightened at the sight of someone who could discuss motorcycles with him. Jennifer had told Lexi many times that one of the reasons she and Matt had become friends was because of the knowledge about motorcycles her father had passed on to her.

When Matt gave Jennifer a twisted half grin—the biggest smile Lexi had ever seen on his face—Minda's face turned a bright, unhealthy shade of red.

"What do you think of her?" he asked Jennifer, with something bordering on enthusiasm.

Before Jennifer could answer, Minda broke in. " 'Her?' Is that what you called your motorcycle? 'Her?' No wonder you haven't got time for other girls—you've got 'her'!"

Jennifer glanced at Minda in surprise. "It's a great bike, Minda. You should see it."

Minda gave Jennifer a stare that could have frozen water. "I don't get my kicks looking at a hunk of machinery, Jennifer. And I certainly wouldn't admit it if I were you!"

Minda turned away and flounced down the hall, her blond hair springing around shoulders rigid with anger.

Jennifer and Matt stared at each other for a moment, then burst out laughing.

"I don't know what that was about, but I wish I did," he chuckled. "See you later, Jen."

As Lexi approached, Jennifer greeted her with a lopsided grin. "Do you know what that was all about?"

"Not exactly, but I think Minda was making a move on Matt, and you got in the middle."

"Oops. Big mistake."

"I agree. Minda was furious. She invited him to a party at her place and he turned her down flat.

Then you came strolling along asking about his bike
and he gave you more attention than Minda's ever
gotten from him."

"Ouch."

"I think you'd better steer clear of Minda for a
couple days," Lexi advised. "Just in case."

———————

Of course, steering clear of Minda wasn't easy.

Lexi, Jennifer, Todd, and Binky were seated in
their usual booth at the Hamburger Shack waiting
for Egg to arrive when Minda sashayed in.

"Oh, oh," Jennifer muttered. "Any room for me
under the table?" She indicated the dark recess beneath them.

"I think I'd rather face Minda. Have you ever
looked at the layers of chewing gum under this table?" Lexi asked cheerfully.

"Gross!" Binky's face crumpled in disgust.

"Maybe you could figure out how to vanish like
Peggy and Chad have been doing lately." Todd suggested. "Has anyone seen them?"

"They were holding hands and strolling off into
the sunset last I saw them. How come they quit coming with us?" Jennifer wondered.

Binky rolled her eyes, "Because they want to be
alone, silly."

"What for? We're more fun than being alone!"

"Being alone together isn't like being *alone* alone,
you know."

"Do you want to translate that?" Todd said with
a smirk.

"Oh, quit teasing!"

Lexi was only half listening to the playful banter

around her. She watched as Minda made her way to the pinball machines where Matt was intent on a game.

Minda sidled up to him and whispered something in his ear. He didn't turn his head, but Lexi could see his eyes narrow. Apparently Minda was implementing a new scheme to entice Matt to her party.

"Number one eighty-five is ready." The call came over the loudspeaker.

"That's our food," Jennifer announced. "I'm on the outside, so I'll go get it." She slid out of the booth and made a bee-line for the counter. Unfortunately, she had to pass by Minda on her way.

Lexi saw Minda's loafer-clad foot edge out into Jennifer's pathway. Jennifer did not.

She sprawled in a loose-limbed heap at the foot of the counter, taking a dispenser of napkins and a salt and pepper shaker from the nearest table with her as she fell.

There was a moment of shocked silence in the Hamburger Shack, then a soft chuckle of laughter that quickly built into a roar. Jennifer shook her head and looked up blankly, still not quite sure what had happened. Then her eyes narrowed as her gaze fell on Minda.

Minda, however, had managed to paste an innocent expression on her features.

"Poor Jennifer!" she said loudly. "Isn't it terrible to be clumsy?"

Jennifer scrambled to her feet. Dusting off her knees, she muttered, "I'd rather be clumsy than mean."

Minda gave her a sweet smile. "I'm *so* glad I'm neither."

A surge of admiration for Jennifer swelled through Lexi as Jennifer gave Minda a weak smile. "Yeah, right." Lexi could imagine how much self-control it had taken for Jennifer not to lash back.

Matt Windsor watched the entire scene with amusement. He'd even stopped playing pinball long enough to lean against the machine and study the two girls.

When Jennifer stomped by carrying the full tray of food from their order, Minda stepped neatly backward out of her way.

Jennifer's face was still pink when she slammed the tray onto the table.

"That little—"

"You were great, Jen. You kept your cool," Lexi hastened to assure her.

"Right. Great," Jennifer agreed sarcastically. "She tripped me, didn't she?"

"You're competition," Todd murmured by way of explanation. "One way to get rid of competition is to make fools of them."

Jennifer groaned and leaned backward in the vinyl seat. "But I'm *not* competition!"

"Tell Minda that," Binky pointed out. "And see if she believes it." She stabbed a french fry into the puddle of ketchup she'd spread on her plate. "And then tell me why my brother is so crazy about her."

"I think we've all come to the conclusion that Minda's behavior is not exactly acceptable to us. But I'm not going to let her ruin my food!" Lexi reached for the burger she'd ordered. She was tired of talking about Minda.

"I'm with Lexi," Todd agreed. "She'd get too much satisfaction if we sat here glaring at her. Pass the salt and pepper, please."

For the next few moments, everyone's attention turned to the food they were eating and the company they kept instead of Minda and the dark-haired boy across the room.

Suddenly Binky glanced up and said, "Well, well, well. Looks like whatever she did worked."

Lexi looked up to see Minda and Matt walking toward the front door together. On the street in front of the building was a group of young men on motorcycles. It occurred to Lexi that she wouldn't like to meet any of them while alone on a dark street. But Minda glowed triumphantly as she swung onto the back of Matt's motorcycle and tucked her hands cozily around his waist.

He kicked back the stand, revved the motor to life and they careened away down the street, Matt's dark hair and Minda's pale blond tresses ruffling in the wind.

The foursome inside the Hamburger Shack was silent.

It was Todd who broke the silence by crumpling his paper malt cup into a ball and shooting it toward the garbage can. "Maybe she and Matt are meant for each other," he observed dryly. "They both certainly know how to make trouble."

Chapter Five

They both certainly know how to make trouble.

Todd's comment echoed through Lexi's mind all the way home from the Hamburger Shack.

Was that what Minda found attractive about Matt—his sullenness, his "bad boy" image? Was he Minda's way of rebelling and drawing more attention to herself?

Lexi, always interested in the "whys" and "hows" of people's personalities, was thoughtful as she and Todd mounted the steps of the Leighton house.

"You're not saying very much," Todd observed gently. Lexi knew, however, that silences never bothered him. It was one of the reasons they could be so comfortable together. He offered her time to think.

"I'm still thinking about that scene with Minda and Jennifer. I'm amazed that Jennifer didn't bop Minda on the head."

Todd nodded. "Jennifer has come a long way this year." Then he frowned. "And Minda seems to be regressing."

Lexi held open the screen door. "Want to come inside for a while?"

41

"Half an hour. Mike's got work for me at the garage." Todd often worked for his older brother after school when there were extra jobs.

After they were settled in the living room, Todd on the couch, Lexi in the easy chair across from him, she voiced the question she'd had all afternoon.

"Todd, you told me once that Matt didn't always used to be a troublemaker. What happened?"

Todd kicked off his shoes and stretched out across the davenport. He rested his head on crisscrossed arms and propped his feet on the arm of the couch. "I asked my mom about it last night. I figured she might know something more than I do about Matt."

Mrs. Winston was a well-respected business-woman in Cedar River. She oversaw Camp Courage, a camp for the handicapped, and was well known for her skill at writing grants for special funding. It was true that she seemed to have her finger on the pulse of the entire Cedar River community.

"And?" Lexi tucked her legs beneath her and tugged at the hem of the Scotch plaid skirt she'd sewn.

"And she told me some stuff about Matt's family that I'd never known."

"What did she say?"

"That when Matt and I first knew each other, his mom was still living with their family."

"You said she'd moved to Canada and taken Matt's sister with her."

"Yeah . . . Apparently Matt's father was . . . you know . . . fooling around."

"Oh."

"Anyway, they got a divorce and Matt stayed with his father."

"So he used to have a whole family and now it's just Matt and his dad?" No wonder he looked so grim sometimes!

"For a while. Then his dad remarried."

Lexi curled a little deeper into her chair. "How long ago was that?"

"About three years ago. I guess that's when Matt started to change. They moved to a new neighborhood and I didn't see much of him."

"I suppose it was hard to have his father bring home a new wife," Lexi mused. "I can't even imagine how I'd feel about it."

Todd nodded grimly. "Especially if she were only a few years older than you."

"Huh?" Lexi straightened in her chair. "Why'd you say that?"

"Mom told me that Matt's father married a 'younger woman.' I guess Matt and his new mom are only about ten years apart in age."

Lexi swallowed hard. "Todd, where does Matt live now?"

"Somewhere over on Willard Avenue."

"Do you know what his new mom looks like?"

Todd shook his head thoughtfully. "I think my mother said she was tiny and blond but I can't remember. Why?"

Lexi stared reflectively out the window. "I was delivering something for my dad the other day when I got lost and ended up on Willard. I saw Matt in front of a house talking to a girl. At least I *thought* it was a girl. She could have been older. Maybe it was his stepmother."

"Well, at least they were talking," Todd answered

hopefully. "According to Mom, they don't do much of that with each other."

"Well, they weren't exactly *talking*."

"What do you mean?"

"Fighting was more like it." Lexi paused before adding, "I saw her slap Matt."

Todd whistled through his teeth. "What did he do?"

"Nothing. His shoulders just sagged and he turned away."

"Doesn't sound like Matt." Todd's brow furrowed.

"What could he do? She's his stepmother!"

"True." Todd leaned back into the pillows. "No wonder he's so touchy. I think I would be too."

"Do you think that's the reason for the wild hair and the black leather?" Lexi asked. "To get back at his dad?"

Todd shrugged and ran his fingers through his blond hair. "It's all too complicated for me." He glanced at his watch and swung his feet off the couch. "I've got to go to work. Mike will be waiting."

"Thanks for walking me home," Lexi murmured. "I appreciated the company."

"Anytime. You know that." Todd studied her for a long minute and then chucked her gently under the chin. "Don't look so glum. Matt will have to work things out for himself." He grinned impishly. "And so will Minda—unless Jennifer gets to her first."

Lexi gave a thin smile. She worried about people, that was all. She couldn't help it. She seemed to have an overdeveloped sensitivity to people who were hurting. Often she found herself hurting with them.

Her dad called it the "stray cat syndrome." Every time she found a stray animal—cat, dog, bird, or even once, a guinea pig—she wanted to take it home and nurse it back to health. It happened with stray people too. She found herself wanting to help Matt. In her mind she saw him as a younger boy, missing his mother and confused by his father's behavior, not the sullen, forbidding person he was now.

A smile curved the corners of Todd's lips. "I can almost read that mind of yours, Lexi. 'Poor Matt,' it's thinking. 'No wonder he's been acting so rotten. I wonder how I can help.' Right?"

"All right, Mr. Smart Guy. Just because you can read minds doesn't mean your brother will let you be late for work!"

They both laughed as Lexi walked Todd to the door. When he'd disappeared down the steps and through the gate, she returned to the chair in the living room, curled into a tight ball on the seat and closed her eyes.

What if *her* mother had left and taken Ben with her?

What if *her* father brought home a woman less than thirty years old and said this was to be her new mother?

What if . . .

Lexi shook her head. It was too difficult to imagine. She was relieved to hear Ben and her mother enter the back door with a loud crash of the screen door and the thump of groceries being settled onto the table.

———

Minda was engaged in all-out battle. Matt Windsor was her goal, and every girl in school who'd ever looked at him twice was her enemy.

"Have you seen Minda today?" Binky gasped into Lexi's ear. "I mean have you *seen* her?"

"Yes, Bink. Twice." Lexi tried to be patient. She was sick and tired of having conversations about Minda Hannaford's new wardrobe.

It was apparent that Minda had set out to make a conquest. The challenge was Matt Windsor; the tool: black leather. She was wearing a short, tight mini-skirt of black leather, an oversized T-shirt with the words "School Stinks" on the front, and short black boots with tiny silver studs.

Ever since the night she and Matt had driven away together from the Hamburger Shack, they'd been a twosome. It was more by Minda's design than Matt's, Lexi concluded. She'd even seen Matt duck into an empty room to avoid Minda in the hallway. Still, when Minda was with him—practically glued to his elbow—he didn't seem to mind. He treated Minda as he did most of the girls in school—as if they didn't exist.

Occasionally, though, he would smile or talk to her, and Minda's face would light up like the Christmas tree on the White House lawn.

As far as Lexi could see, Matt and Minda seemed to be on some sort of out-of-control downward spiral.

"Well, I think she looks stupid," Binky concluded to no one in particular. "Especially in those boots."

Lexi laughed. She liked crazy clothing herself, so it was difficult to fault Minda for that. "There's nothing we can do about Minda's new wardrobe, Binky, so I guess we shouldn't worry about it."

"True," Binky acquiesced. She straightened her tiny frame and added, "Anyway, Peggy and Chad aren't acting much better."

Lexi frowned. Now *that* was a couple she felt a little bit responsible for.

"Binky, do you see much of Peggy?"

"Not lately. Not unless she's draped all over Chad." Binky stuck out her tongue. "Yuk."

Lexi couldn't help nodding. She'd thought the same thing. The romance between Peggy and Chad had been thickening all fall. Now Peggy hardly spent any time with her other friends unless, of course, Chad was in tow. More and more they wanted to spend time alone together.

"Do you like Chad?" Binky wondered aloud to Lexi. "I mean, really *like* him?"

"I don't know him that well, Binky. I'm new here, remember?"

Binky gave a wide smile. "I keep forgetting that. It seems to me that you've lived in Cedar River forever."

"Thanks, I think."

"He seems nice," Binky continued. "And he's cute enough. Maybe I just don't like that he monopolizes so much of Peggy's time."

"She doesn't seem to mind," Lexi pointed out, trying to be fair. "Just because we wouldn't do it—"

"You mean *couldn't* do it. My dad tells me I can't date until I'm thirty-six!" Binky threw herself against a locker to dramatize her point.

Lexi laughed. "And I thought my parents were tough!"

Binky gave a nonchalant little shrug. "It's more fun this way, anyway. I'd rather be with our group than wandering off together like Peggy and Chad." She wrinkled her nose into a mask of disgust. "But have you seen them in the hallways making fools of themselves?"

"Fools? How?"

Binky threw her hands over her heart and her head back. She rolled and fluttered her eyes and made kissing sounds with her mouth. "Don't you see them separating for class? You'd think Chad was going on a moon expedition instead of typing class!"

Lexi *had* noticed, but she hadn't wanted to say anything. She remained silent.

Binky was not so reserved. "I think it's sick. Somebody should talk to them about it! Tell them how dumb it looks." Then her pale eyes began to flicker. "*You* should tell them, Lexi!"

"Me? Oh no . . ." Lexi took a step backward. The last thing she wanted to do was make Peggy angry. Peggy Madison was one of her first and very best friends in Cedar River. She didn't want to do anything to change that.

Binky let the subject drop as they made their way to class, but Lexi couldn't quit thinking about what Binky had said. Somebody should talk to Peggy. Anybody. Anybody but her.

———

It always seemed that when she fought something she was meant to do, things fell into place anyway. Lexi firmly believed that God had a hand on her shoulder, steering her the way she should go. That thought occurred to Lexi as she left school that afternoon and within minutes Peggy Madison fell in step beside her.

"What? No Chad?" Lexi teased gently.

"He's got a dental appointment." Her mouth drooped unhappily.

"I see."

Peggy helped her answer the question. "It's crazy, but I miss him already!" She blushed to a rosy pink. "It's terrible having to be apart."

Lexi gave her a sideways glance. "Even for classes?"

Peggy rolled her eyes. "We should have planned better. We could have shared a lot more of them if we'd only known . . ." Her voice trailed away.

"Known how serious you were going to get about each other?"

"Yeah." Peggy looked dreamy-eyed. "Great, isn't it?"

"You're awfully young, Peg," Lexi ventured, wincing at how much she sounded like her mother.

Peggy looked at her sharply, immediately on the defensive. "Are you trying to tell me something, Lexi?"

"Not really. It's just that my dad doesn't let me go out unless it's a whole group."

"Yeah? I guess that's fun too, but Chad and I . . ." She blushed again. "We just like to be alone. Like I said, I even hate to say goodbye between classes."

"So I've noticed," Lexi muttered, not meaning for Peggy to hear.

"And what is *that* supposed to mean?"

Lexi drew a deep breath. *Here goes*, she thought to herself. "Well, sometimes you and Chad make a pretty big scene. It's embarrassing, I guess, to watch you hugging and kissing in the hallways, that's all."

"That's all!" Peggy's blush turned to a full-fledged, mottled anger on her cheeks. "It's none of your business what Chad and I do between classes!"

"I just mean that maybe you should save some stuff for private. I didn't—"

"I know what you meant, Lexi. But you don't understand. Chad and I are in *love*. We *need* to be together."

Lexi could see that Peggy was furious. She laid a hand on her friend's arm. "I'm sorry, Peggy. Maybe I was out of line. If I hurt your feelings, I'm sorry. I guess I thought I was helping, not hurting you."

Peggy faltered and the redness faded a bit from her cheeks. "Yeah, well, meddling doesn't help."

Lexi accepted the criticism. This wasn't worth losing Peggy's friendship over. "I really am sorry. Forgive me?"

Peggy gave a weak smile. Then she flung her arm around Lexi's shoulders. "Sure, why not? I know you'd never intentionally hurt anyone, Lexi." She paused. "It's just that you don't understand about Chad and me, that's all. Just wait. Someday you will."

When the two girls parted, they were both smiling, but Lexi's smile was a false one. She'd tried and failed. At what, she wasn't quite sure. She didn't want Peggy and Chad to break up. Maybe she just wanted them to realize that they shouldn't be so tied up in each other that they cut off all their old friends.

Lexi breathed a deep, gusty sigh. Life was just too complicated. Then her face lifted in a smile. She knew just the antidote for her depression. She'd go home and play with Ben.

Chapter Six

It was a particularly quiet Saturday. Ben and Mrs. Leighton had gone shopping, and Lexi's father was finishing up some paperwork at the veterinary clinic. By noon, Lexi had already rearranged her furniture twice, cleaned her drawers and finished her homework for Monday. She was pleased to hear the telephone ring.

"Hello, Leighton residence."

"Hi, Lexi," the familiar voice on the other end of the line said. "What are you doing today?"

"Todd!" Lexi exclaimed delightedly. "Nothing, nothing at all. I'm just about bored out of my head."

"I'm down at Mike's garage and he's gone out on a call, so I can't leave. Any chance you'd make me a tuna fish sandwich, bring it down here and keep me company while I eat?"

Lexi laughed. "Why, I think there's a very good chance of that, Todd. I've been looking for something to do."

"Great. Use plenty of mayo, okay? And if you have any of those chocolate chip cookies your mother makes—"

"Yes, Todd. I'll bring you a gourmet lunch straight from the Leighton kitchen."

"Good girl," he chuckled and his voice warmed the line. "I knew I was calling the right one when I called you. Thanks, Lexi. See you in a little bit."

"Bye."

She was still smiling when she hung up. Crazy Todd. Sweet, funny, crazy Todd.

She rubbed her hands on the legs of her jeans as she entered the kitchen. Todd had called just in time. Her own stomach was beginning to growl with hunger. While she hadn't felt like cooking only for herself, a picnic for two would be great fun. Industriously, she made the sandwiches, washed the fruit and packed everything in a brown paper sack, quickly cleaning up the kitchen before she left.

It was nice to feel useful, especially after the bad scene she'd had with Peggy the other afternoon. That little incident hadn't done much for Lexi's self-confidence where her friends were concerned.

At the garage, Lexi found Todd in the back working on his own car, a vintage '49 Ford coupe he was restoring to its former splendor. Todd was lovingly polishing some of the chrome grillwork on the front of the car.

"Looking good, Todd!" Lexi exclaimed.

"Thanks. If I can have about five more minutes without a customer, I'll have this done."

Lexi settled the bag of sandwiches on a tool-littered table. "Why don't I go out front and try to keep them away," Lexi offered cheerfully. "You keep polishing."

In about three minutes, Todd emerged from the back room. "All done. Let's eat." He was wiping his hands on a greasy towel strung from his belt and he'd managed to get smudge marks on both cheeks, his chin, his T-shirt, and his knee.

"You look like you need a bath more than lunch," Lexi said cheerfully.

"Well, my stomach thinks otherwise. Whad'ja bring me?"

Together they spread out sandwiches, fruit and cookies on a small table in the back and began to eat. After Todd's third sandwich, he relaxed enough to begin visiting.

"This was great, Lexi. Thanks, I really appreciate it."

"Anytime. Lexi's catering service is open twenty-four hours a day."

"But I don't think your answering service—I mean your dad—is open that many hours a day."

Lexi chuckled, "Probably not. My dad is pretty strict about phone calls. The other night he—"

Both Todd and Lexi heard the bell ring at the front of the shop. That meant someone had entered the building. Todd jumped up and raced for the front with Lexi close on his heels. Then his steps slowed. They were both surprised to see Matt Windsor standing in the doorway, his feet wide-spread and his hands on his hips, glancing around the building.

"Hi. Is Mike here?" he asked.

"No, not right now. What can I do for you?" Todd offered.

"I just wanted to pull in and use a couple of his tools on my bike," Matt said casually. "Do you think he'd mind?"

Todd glanced around. His brother Mike was normally very generous with his tools. He didn't see why

Mike would view Matt differently than any of the other boys that came from the school to work on their cars occasionally.

"Sure, help yourself." Todd gave an apologetic smile. "Lexi and I were just eating lunch."

Matt was already deeply engrossed in his search for the right tool. He waved Lexi and Todd away with his hand. "Go on, finish eating. Don't pay any attention to me."

Todd nodded and backed toward the door that led into the back room. "Sure, well, help yourself. We're right here if you need anything."

Once he was in the privacy of the back room with Lexi, she whispered, "Do you think you should have let him do that?"

Todd shrugged. "I don't see why not. Mike's always letting someone use his tools. Matt's no different than anyone else."

Lexi gave him a doubtful look. "I wouldn't say that if I were you."

Todd grinned. "True. I guess you'd say Matt is like *no one* else. Still, that doesn't mean he can't use my brother's tools."

Slowly, they finished the last of the cookies and split the final orange before considering their lunch officially over. Then Todd moved toward the pop machine. "Want to split a can?" he asked.

"Sure, why not?" Lexi leaned back and propped her feet on the littered table. *It is wonderfully relaxing spending the afternoon here with Todd,* she thought. *And so much less boring than being at home rattling around in an empty house.*

The two of them talked about school, the Emerald Tones and their plans for photos in the upcoming issues of the school newspaper. When Todd glanced at his watch, his eyebrows arched in surprise. "Whoa! It's getting late. I didn't realize what time it is. My brother will be back pretty soon. I'd better get out front."

Lexi nodded and moved to pick up the litter of papers between them. She deposited them in the garbage can and followed Todd out the door into the main room of the shop.

Matt's bike was still in the garage, but Matt himself was nowhere to be seen. Todd glanced around. "I wonder where he went. He wouldn't have just left without his bike. Maybe he . . ." Todd paused to sniff the air. "Do you smell something funny in here, Lexi?"

Lexi wrinkled her nose and said, "Oil, grease, gasoline. Maybe a little incense."

"One thing I can tell you for sure, my brother *does not* burn incense in his garage." Todd's expression grew grim. "Where's Matt? We've got to find him, Lexi."

Just then, Matt came strolling out of the men's restroom, the butt of a cigarette dangling half in and half out of his lips.

"What do you think you're doing, Windsor?" Todd yelled angrily.

Lexi wondered what had made his mood alter so radically and so quickly.

"What's your problem, Todd?" Matt asked nonchalantly. "Can't a guy go in the bathroom and—"

"No, not if that's what you're going to do."

Lexi looked blankly at Todd, then at Matt, then back to Todd again. What were they talking about?

"Get rid of it." Todd's voice was grim and trembling with anger.

Matt eyed him for a moment, one eyebrow arched defiantly. "Get rid of what?"

"Whatever it is you're smoking in there. My brother doesn't approve of that sort of thing and I don't want it in his shop."

"You trying to accuse me of something, Winston?" Matt said with a sneer on his face. "Sweet little Todd Winston trying to tell me that I'm doing something wrong? Can it be?"

Lexi didn't like the snide, sneering tone in Matt's voice. For an instant, she realized just how naive she had been.

That wasn't incense she could smell in the shop mingling with the fumes of motor oil and solvents; it was the sickly, sweet smell of marijuana. Lexi tried to remember the odor. At Grover Point, two policemen had come to school one day and given a demonstration on drugs and how to identify them. Lexi remembered being warned about the sweet, musky odor of marijuana. "Smells a lot like incense," one of the policemen had said.

"Get out, Matt. You're done working in here today." Todd's tone was clipped and furious. "My brother left me in charge here and I can't allow you to do that."

Matt dropped the dangling cigarette butt to the floor and ground it out with the toe of his boot. "Hey, I'm not done, Todd. I just got started."

"No. That's where you're wrong. You're done. Now! Get out." Todd advanced toward Matt with a threatening step, his fists clenched, his eyes blue and stormy like the ocean.

"I won't get out. I'm not done with my bike. You said I could work here and—"

"That was before I caught you smoking grass in my brother's shop. You knew that Mike wouldn't approve of that. You broke the rules here. Now it's time for you to leave. Out, Matt." Todd lifted his arm and gave Matt a little shove, pressing his fingers into the line of his shoulder blade.

"I said I'm not done." Matt lifted his arm and pushed Todd back.

First he pushed lightly, then harder, and harder still until Todd stumbled backward and caught himself against the fender of a car.

"You don't push me around in here, Matt. Stop it and get out."

"Why should I listen to you?" Matt said scornfully, advancing step by step toward Todd. "What makes you think you can make me get out?"

The two boys faced off. Matt pushed against Todd's shoulder. "Come on. Come on. Make me. Just make me leave. I'd like to see you try it."

Much to Lexi's amazement, Todd lifted his arm and pushed back. "I want you out. Now."

Returning the shove force-for-force, Matt once again pushed Todd. "It's a free country. If I want to be in here, I'll be in here."

"This is private property," Todd retorted.

"Well, then, I'm gonna wait until whoever owns this property comes to tell me I can't be on it. I don't have to listen to you."

Lexi glanced at her watch. When was it that Mike had said he'd be back to the store? Soon, she hoped. Very, very soon.

"I'm doing you a favor, Matt," Todd said in a low voice. "If my brother comes back and catches you here and finds out that you were smoking a joint, he'll—"

Just then, Matt's arm shot out and gave Todd a forceful shove, which sent him spinning and reeling toward a workbench. Todd caught himself in time, shook his head, and stomped back toward Matt.

"What d'ya think you're doing? You can't just push me around like that."

"Wanna bet?" Matt snapped. There was a grim, pleased smile on his face, which Lexi had never seen before. It gave her a chill. Matt wanted to fight. He was enjoying this, Lexi could see it in his eyes. Matt's fist shot out and landed square in Todd's stomach. Lexi heard the breath leave him and the soft painful "oomph" sound of a fist in the belly. Todd staggered a bit, then recovered and returned with a jab of his own. Within a second, the disagreement had escalated into an out-and-out brawl between the two boys. Finally, Todd threw himself against Matt's shoulder with all the force he could muster and the two boys fell to the floor, kicking, pounding, and clawing.

"No!" Lexi cried. "Don't do that. Stop! Please stop!" She ran to where the two were flailing and struggling together on the floor. A little trickle of blood flowed from the corner of Todd's lip and there was an angry cut on Matt's cheek. They were going to hurt themselves even worse if they didn't stop this nonsense. Without thinking, Lexi leaned over and grabbed Matt's arm to pull him away from Todd.

Matt, in the heat of the moment, was furious with the intrusion. He flung his arm backward, knocking Lexi off balance. She staggered, fell into a tool bench and slid down to the floor in a crumpled heap.

"Ow" was the painful little moan that slipped from between her lips. The little moan did more to snap the two boys to their senses than any amount of tugging and pulling or pleading Lexi could have done.

Todd pushed himself away from Matt and was at her side. "Lexi, are you all right? Did he hurt you?"

"Hurt her? Hey, I didn't mean to—"

"Well, you saw her fall, didn't you? That was your doing."

Matt's eyes flashed. "I didn't mean to push her down. She just got in the way and—"

"Is that what you do to everyone who gets in your way, Windsor? Do you just push them around, push them away, not caring if they get hurt? If that's your style, it's a pretty lousy one." Then Todd turned his disdainful expression away from Matt.

Gently, Todd helped Lexi to her feet. She was fine, she decided, except for an irritating wobbliness in her knees and a bit of a pain in her back where the corner of the table had stabbed at her.

"I'm okay, Todd. Really." She tried to brush off his worried touches and gestures, but she could see in his eyes that he was furious.

Matt moved slowly to his feet. "Are you sure you're all right, Lexi? I really didn't mean to . . ."

Lexi made her way to the chair. She was surprised to find herself limping. Perhaps she had twisted her ankle as she had fallen. There seemed to be a sharp pain radiating upward from her heel and into her calf.

"She's hurt, Windsor. Are you happy, now? Are you happy about that?" Todd taunted, his fists still clenching and unclenching furiously.

Matt looked with anguished eyes from Todd to Lexi, then back to Todd again. Without another word, he walked to his bike, pushed down the kick-stand and rolled it out of the shop.

When Mike returned to the shop a few moments later, he found Todd and Lexi huddled together around the chair, Todd's face furious, Lexi's washed with some tears of pain.

"What's going on in here?" he demanded. "How come I just saw Windsor racing down the street like a posse was chasing him and now I find you two in here and Lexi's crying and . . . what's going on?"

Lexi pleaded to Todd with her eyes. *Don't tell.* She'd gotten in the way. It hadn't been her fight. She realized that. And anyway, Matt had enough troubles without getting a reputation for knocking girls down as well. Maybe Matt didn't care, but there was an anguished look in his eye that seemed to tell her that he really did. "I think I sprained my ankle, Mike. Something really dumb, huh?"

Mike came over and leaned down by Lexi's chair and fingered the throbbing ankle with a gentle touch. "Doesn't feel like anything's broken, but maybe you should go home and put it up for a few hours. Do you have an ice bag?"

Lexi nodded weakly. "Sure do. No problem. I'll just be going now." She tried to stand up, but her ankle gave a twinge.

"Come here," Todd said gruffly. With that, he bent over, tucked his right arm beneath her knees and his left arm around her shoulders and picked her up. "I'll carry you home since you can't walk on that ankle."

"Oh, that's not necessary . . ." she began.

But of course, it was. The ankle was hurting. There was no way she was going to make it from the garage to her home on the painful ankle tonight. With some ice and a little rest it would be fine, she told herself. The ankle would heal—but she couldn't say the same for the hurt deep within Matt.

Chapter Seven

"Play with me, Lexi?" Ben pleaded. He had a ball under one arm and his button box clutched tightly in his little fist. "Play with Ben?"

"Ben, we've been playing all afternoon," Lexi groaned. "You've worn me out." It was a week since Lexi's confrontation with Matt. They'd been playing for four hours straight, ever since Mr. and Mrs. Leighton had gone shopping for a new living room couch.

To Ben, however, it hardly seemed reason to be tired.

"Why don't you go and eat one of those brownies on the kitchen table," Lexi suggested hopefully. "Do you want me to get you a glass of milk?"

"Milk," Ben echoed firmly. "Milk and brownie."

In the kitchen, Lexi glanced at the large clock on the wall. Surely, a davenport couldn't be that hard to find. Her mother and dad should be back any minute now. Baby-sitting for Ben was one of Lexi's favorite pastimes, but he'd learned so many new games and activities at school that he kept her racing every minute of their time together. At least for the moment, he was happily munching on a thick chocolate brownie and watching a cartoon on television.

Lexi wandered back into the living room to pick up the pieces of the games and puzzles they'd been using. She glanced out the window, but the Leighton car was nowhere in sight. She decided that if Ben insisted she put together one more puzzle or color one more page of a coloring book, her eyes were going to fall right out of her head. Lexi felt more than just a little relief when she heard the doorbell ring.

Her parents must have locked themselves out. Quickly, she crossed the living room and foyer to open the front door. She was startled to see Matt Windsor on the other side of the screen door.

"Matt!" she blurted. "What are you doing here?"

He stood on the top step shifting his weight uncomfortably from one foot to the other.

"Well, what are you doing here?" Lexi demanded again. She was in no mood to see Matt. She was still stiff and sore from her encounter with him the week before.

As she eyed him from head to toe, she decided she wasn't about to let him get by easily for what had happened last Saturday in Mike Winston's garage. Besides, Matt's sullen, almost pouting expression was making her feel uncomfortable.

"I want to talk—inside." He said it in a tone that made Lexi think he was unaccustomed to being defied.

A surge of stubbornness swelled in Lexi. She didn't want to talk to Matt. Not after last Saturday. She really didn't even want to see him. With her right hand, she began to push the door closed. As she did so, she caught a glimpse of the expression in his eyes. There was nothing wild or evil there. Instead, she saw other emotions, like hurt, or anger, and perhaps a little regret. Lexi put out a hand to stop the door from closing any farther.

Matt sensed her hesitation, took a small step forward toward the screen door through which he viewed her. "Please? I really need to talk to you."

A strand of dark hair fell into a curl over his forehead, and the dusky lash-fringed eyes widened. Lexi's resolve weakened. He reminded her of someone. Who was it? Just then, Ben's small treble voice came floating from the kitchen.

"Row, row, row your boat, gently down the stream; merrily, merrily, merrily, merrily. . . ."

As she stared at Matt, the thought struck her. Matt reminded her of Ben. The first days after they had moved to Cedar River, he had been so lonely, so hurt, so confused. Ben and Matt shared the same expression in their eyes.

Impulsively, before she could think it through or change her mind, Lexi pushed open the door. "Come in."

He glided through the door and stood waiting in the hallway until Lexi gestured him into the living room. Already she was regretting her action. Matt was a discomforting presence here, a dark cloud on a sunny day, a shadow on the bright ambience of the room.

He prowled the living room like a caged panther, looking at everything as he paced the perimeter, but touching nothing. His eyes moved rapidly from side to side and up and down as if he were memorizing every nook and cranny, every picture and pillow, every drape and rug. As Lexi watched, he moved stealthily around the room once and then a second time before pausing to stop in front of her in the middle of the room.

"Well," she managed to stammer. "What do you want?"

His eyes flickered and he licked his lips, but he did not answer. Instead, he walked toward the five-tiered bookcase in the corner of the room on which Lexi's mother kept family photos. The thought of Matt studying those pictures with such a cold and calculating eye made Lexi shiver. She stepped forward, eager to distract his attention from what suddenly seemed so private and so personal.

Before she reached him, Matt picked up a family picture the Leightons had taken just prior to leaving Grover's Point. It rested in a dainty oval brass frame, and Mrs. Leighton had lovingly added a ruffle of lace to the outside edge of the picture. The photo was one of Lexi's favorites. Her memories of the day it was taken were some of her best. Ben had just celebrated his birthday and she had been chosen cheerleader for the following season. Of course, Lexi had not known then that she would have to leave Grover's Point and come to Cedar River.

"Isn't this sweet?" Matt sneered. "One little, happy family."

Lexi grabbed the picture out of his hand. "Put that back. You can't come into my house and make fun of what we have here."

"Who said I was making fun?" Matt retorted. "It's just that everything that's here is so sweet, it's a little bit sickening. Don't you get sick and tired of being nice all the time, Lexi? And having perfect parents? And—"

She interrupted his comments. "We're far from perfect, Matt. But one thing we aren't, is rude."

"Well, isn't it wonderful that Lexi Leighton and her family aren't rude?" He was sneering now and moving again around the room. "Not only are the Leightons, especially Lexi, perfect, but they're also polite."

"Far from perfect, Matt," Lexi said through gritted teeth. "But, then again, you don't know anything about us."

"Oh, I can tell," he gestured wildly with his arm. "Perfect little family on a perfect little street in a perfect little house with no problems in the world to bother them—"

Just then, Ben entered the room carrying his button box and his ball. "Brownies gone, Lexi. Play with me?" Ben skidded to a halt right at Matt's feet. Ben's little white tennis shoes touched the toes of Matt's black boots. "Will you play with me?" Ben inquired politely.

"Who's this?" Matt asked gruffly.

"This is Ben, my little brother," Lexi answered. She took Ben by the shoulders, spun him around and steered him back toward the kitchen. "I have company now, Ben. You'll have to go outside and play."

"Can't he play with me?" Ben inquired, pointing with his stubby finger over his shoulder.

"No, Ben. Matt came to see me. Why don't you go look at the bunnies," Lexi suggested, referring to the two lop-eared rabbits her father had brought home from the office one evening. "See if the bunnies need any lettuce."

"Okay," Ben agreed cheerfully.

He shuffled off happily to the backyard via the

vegetable crisper in the refrigerator. When Lexi turned again to face Matt, he had a quizzical look in his eyes.

"Guess things aren't as perfect as I thought," he remarked.

Lexi's eyebrow arched in surprise. "What makes you say that?"

"Your little brother. He's—"

"Retarded?" Lexi finished for him.

"Yeah, I'm sorry about what I said. I didn't know."

"Ben's okay," Lexi said briefly. "There's no need to apologize."

Suddenly Matt's head dropped and his whole demeanor changed entirely. "Oh yes, there is. There's lots for me to apologize for." His sudden change of attitude was as startling as the moment when Lexi had found him on her doorstep.

Lexi could think of nothing to do but gesture toward the couch and say, "Want to sit down?"

Matt moved toward the davenport. He flung himself into its corner and sat there tapping the floor with his foot in a nervous rhythm.

"So then, what was it you wanted to say?" Lexi asked. She seated herself firmly on the edge of a wing-backed chair, her hands on her knees, her back rigid and stiff.

"I'm sorry," Matt started. "I'm sorry about what happened in Mike's shop last week. I'm sorry about what I just said." His beautiful brown eyes flickered. "That's why I usually don't talk. When I do, I get it all . . . wrong." Lexi was silent and he finally continued. "I didn't hurt you or anything, did I? I mean, I've never done anything like that before. I really would feel terrible if I hurt you."

Lexi thought gingerly of a couple sore spots she'd noticed, but she smiled as she answered, "Nothing serious. I'm okay, Matt."

The hurt, regret and bitterness in his eyes was almost more than Lexi could bear. "I think I understand, Matt. Todd tried to explain to me how things were for you."

He looked up. A humorless smile twisted one corner of his lip. "Yeah? Todd's a good guy, Lexi. He's defended me a lot of times when he probably shouldn't have."

"He said things were hard for you at home and maybe that's why you—"

"Things hard for me? at home?" He gave a harsh laugh. "They aren't hard—they're impossible."

"So? Tell me about it."

Matt glanced at her in surprise. "You don't want to know."

"Let me decide that," Lexi shot back. "It's the least I deserve after being practically knocked through a garage wall."

Matt's head hung even lower. "My mom would kill me if she knew that I hit a girl." His voice was soft and far away.

"Where is your mom?" Lexi asked quietly, remembering what Todd had said about the family.

"Canada," he finally murmured. "With my little sister."

"Do you miss them?" Lexi asked, not quite sure what else to say.

When Matt raised his head to look at her, his eyes were gleaming with pain. "Miss them? I miss them every minute of every day." Then his eyes darkened and flashed. "I hate them, too. They had no right to leave."

"Todd told me you have a stepmother, Matt. What about her?"

"Lorilee, you mean?" He sneered.

"Is she so bad?" Lexi murmured, the image in her mind of Matt being slapped by a tiny, youthful blond woman.

"My father doesn't think so." He gave a short laugh. "Of course, I probably don't either. After all, Lorilee and I are only about ten years apart in age. Kinda funny, you know. Sometimes when we go out, people think that Lorilee and I are sister and brother." Matt chuckled cruelly. "That really gets to my dad."

"Is it because she's so young that you don't like her?" Lexi asked.

Matt's eyes shuttered closed. "None of your business."

Lexi sat up a little straighter. "Maybe it is my business, Matt. What did you come here for? You said you wanted to talk. You shoved Todd and I around a week ago in Mike's garage, behaving like a big, overgrown child. Now you've come to my house, saying you want to talk."

"So, we're talking." A glimmer of admiration flickered in Matt's eyes. "You're a tough little cookie, aren't you?"

Ignoring the comment, Lexi asked, "Do you want a glass of lemonade?"

"What, no tea and crumpets?" Matt sneered. Then he caught himself and his cheeks flushed. "I'll take some lemonade. Thanks."

Lexi nodded at him. "That's better. Now you're behaving."

Matt gave a small grin, stood up and followed her into the kitchen. When Lexi turned around, he had made himself at home at the kitchen table. The afternoon sun was shining though the window, making a bright, friendly pattern across the tabletop. She could hear Ben singing in the backyard and smell the pot of vanilla potpourri that was still cooking on the kitchen stove. It was a very cozy scene.

As she set the glass of lemonade in front of Matt, he commented, "It's nice here. I like it."

"I'm sure it's nice at your house, too," Lexi assured him. Then she gave him a quick glance. "That is, of course, if you'd let yourself enjoy it."

"What's that supposed to mean?" he asked. This time there was no defensiveness in his tone, only curiosity.

"I mean, maybe you should try to get along with your stepmother, Lorilee. Maybe you should give your dad a chance and try to understand why they got married."

"And why they drove away my mother and little sister?"

Lexi shrugged, "I don't know anything about that. But, it seems to me, that if this Lorilee is living in your home, you'd better try to make it work."

"Is this a little sermonette from the religious Lexi Leighton?" Matt asked.

Lexi was startled. He shifted from one mood to another with such lightning speed that she was hard-pressed to keep up with him. "There are worse reputations to have than being 'religious,' " she retorted cheerfully. Pointing a finger at him, she said softly, "Like yours, for example."

A grin flashed across Matt's face. "Touché," he

muttered. "Maybe I deserved that, but even your religion isn't going to fix the mess that I'm living in."

Lexi remained silent.

"I'm not that interested in a 'cozy home,' " Matt suddenly announced. "I'm thinking about moving out."

Lexi's eyes widened. "But, Matt, you haven't even finished high school yet."

He shrugged. "So? It's been done before. Anyway, that house is going to be too crowded."

"Three people doesn't sound like much of a crowd," Lexi murmured.

Matt gave her a long, appraising stare. "Three people? No. Maybe not, but when the baby comes—"

"The baby?" Lexi echoed.

"Yeah, can you imagine it? Me, big brother Matt." His chair scraped back from the table with an angry sound and Matt jolted to his feet. "Thanks for the lemonade, kid. Sorry if I messed you up. Gotta go."

The screen door was still shuddering when Lexi got to it, but Matt had already disappeared.

Matt's mother and sister were gone, his father remarried a woman not much older than Matt, and now there was a new baby on the way. Lexi gave a small shudder. No wonder Matt Windsor was rebelling. Lexi didn't blame him. In his shoes, she might have given some thought to rebelling herself.

———

"Why are you standing there looking so funny?" a voice demanded through the screen door. "What's wrong?"

Lexi blinked and glanced up. "Oh! Hi, Peggy. I didn't hear you come up the walk."

"No, I suppose you didn't. You were just standing there with this weird, faraway look on your face. What are you thinking about?"

Lexi managed to smile. "Oh, nothing, I guess. Just about another friend of mine." When the word 'friend' slipped off Lexi's lips, she was surprised to find that she meant it.

She pushed open the screen door and invited Peggy inside. "I haven't seen you forever," she complained, glad for a reason not to think any longer of Matt.

"I know," Peggy groaned and flopped loose-limbed onto the couch. "It's just between schoolwork and Chad, I haven't had very much time to—"

Lexi wiggled a finger in the air. "There's the key word—Chad. That's who's been taking up all the free time that your girlfriends used to get."

Peggy smiled serenely. "Too true, I have to admit." Her eyes took on a gauzy, distant glow. "It's just that it seems like we never have enough time to spend together. Chad is so . . . sweet."

Remembering the unpleasant conversation she'd had with Peggy the other day, Lexi was careful not to get herself into trouble this afternoon. Instead, she offered Peggy a glass of lemonade and a listening ear. It wasn't long before Peggy began to talk.

"You know, Lexi?" she said thoughtfully, "I've been really thinking about my life lately."

Lexi gave a small, indelicate snort. "Haven't we all?" Her own life seemed all tangled up with Matt's at the moment.

"I've been thinking about my future. You know, with Chad."

Lexi's eyebrow arched in surprise. "Seems kind

of early to be thinking about things like that."

Peggy shook her head emphatically. "Not a bit when you find the guy that you know is absolutely perfect for you. Why waste time looking around when the best thing that ever happened to you is right in front of your nose?"

"This sounds serious," Lexi murmured cheerfully, trying to lighten the mood.

But Peggy was serious and wouldn't be distracted. She looked at Lexi, her eyes wide and luminous. "Chad and I are in love, Lexi. We just don't know what to do about it."

Chapter Eight

"Come *on*, Lexi!" Ben insisted, tugging furiously at his sister's shirtsleeve. "Swings!"

"You go ahead, Ben. I'll catch up." Lexi gave him a little shove toward the playground in the center of the park.

She'd volunteered to let Ben run off some of his energy in the park while her parents took a Sunday afternoon nap after church. They'd stayed up half the night rearranging the living room furniture to accommodate the new davenport.

Her watch said 2:00 o'clock. She'd try to give them another half hour before allowing Ben to descend on the household again. With one eye on Ben, she strolled toward a cluster of park benches surrounding a flowerbed.

Only the marigolds remained, a light fall frost had already withered the other flowers. Lexi pulled her jacket more closely around her. It was chilly this afternoon. She, Ben and a lone figure on the park bench seemed to be the only ones in sight.

As she studied the young man on the bench a gasp escaped her. "Matt!"

He looked up with a startled jerk and Lexi realized he was as surprised as she.

"What are you doing here?" he asked gruffly, obviously not thrilled to have company.

"Watching Ben. How about you?"

It was no wonder she hadn't recognized him, Lexi rationalized. He was wearing a chocolate brown cloth jacket over a fisherman's knit sweater and brown cords with white high-topped tennis shoes. It was something Todd might have worn, but hardly the type of outfit she expected to see on Matt.

"Killing time." He scuffed at the ground with the toe of his tennis shoe. He was quiet for a moment, then seemed to decide he was obligated to explain himself. "I'm supposed to visit my grandmother on Sundays in the nursing home." He angled his head toward the east, to the nursing home situated across the street from the park. "She's sleeping so I thought I'd come over here."

"Oh." Lexi plopped down beside him. He didn't look nearly so forbidding as he did in black leather. "You look nice." She hadn't meant to say it, but it came slipping out. Lexi felt like clapping her hand over her mouth.

Much to her surprise, he smiled. "Thanks. This is my go-to-visit-Grandma outfit."

"I like it."

"You would."

She could have taken offense at that but decided not to. There was something comfortable and pleasant about their conversation today and she didn't want to ruin it.

"You should wear that more often."

Matt looked derisive. "I feel like a jerk in these clothes."

"What do you feel like in your other ones?" Lexi asked curiously.

He shrugged. "I dunno. Stronger, I guess. More in charge."

"That's because people think you carry a knife," Lexi observed frankly. "Is that any way to be in charge?"

He studied her for a long moment. "You really lay it on the line, don't you? Do you ever *not* say what's on your mind?"

Lexi grinned. "Nope."

Matt was forced to smile in return. He glanced at his watch. "The nurse said to wait a half hour and come back." He appeared to hope that half hour would move very quickly.

Lexi leaned back and rested her head against the bench. "Did you think about what we said yesterday?" she finally ventured. Discreetly she watched him from the corner of her eye.

Matt's expression darkened. "Think about it? Yeah, I thought about it. But what good does it do?"

"I don't know. Maybe you'll find a way to change and make things better—"

"I can't change, Lexi. I am who I am. This is me, Matt Windsor. That's it."

"You've changed once before. Are you sure *that* isn't the real Matt Windsor—the person you were before?"

"What do you mean?" The question was staccato sharp.

"Todd told me how different you were when he first knew you. He said you weren't a troublemaker then."

Matt frowned so darkly Lexi wished she'd never

brought up the subject. After a long moment he answered.

"My mother lived with us then and that woman wasn't in my dad's life. I *was* different then. But this is me *now*. Take it or leave it."

Matt's bitter indifference to his own situation was almost harder to accept than his anger. He had a right to be angry. No matter how much he acted as if he didn't care, Lexi was sure it was only a mask.

She remembered pretending that it didn't matter that her brother had Down's syndrome, that she didn't care, and that it didn't make a difference in her life. Her guilt had worn at her like a pair of too-tight shoes until she finally accepted Ben's handicap and quit acting as if it didn't matter.

"You could change again, you know."

Matt gave her a disbelieving stare. "I don't understand you, Lexi. What do you get for meddling in my life? What does it matter to you what I think or what I do?"

Lexi was startled by the venom in his words. Maybe Matt didn't carry a knife tucked into his boot, but there was certainly one on the end of his tongue—and perhaps another twisting in his heart.

"Never mind," he ordered abruptly. "Forget it. I don't want to hear any more of that religion stuff if that's all you're going to talk about." He bent over and picked some pebbles from the ground and began throwing them one by one across the grass.

They sat there for a few moments in total silence. Lexi could hear Ben singing off-key from the swings and an occasional car motoring by. Lexi's silence outlasted Matt's.

"How come you're just sitting there?"

"You told me not to talk."

"And you listened?" He snorted. "I thought females never listened to stuff like that."

"You don't know me very well, then, do you?"

He studied her. "No, I guess I don't."

There was a resigned tone in his voice when he added, "You'd better say it, then. Whatever you wanted to say because then you can leave and feel like you've done your duty by lecturing to me."

Lexi chuckled. "You give me too much credit, Matt. I haven't got a lecture prepared. Not even a mini-sermon. Feel better?"

"What have you got then?"

"Just a bit of information you don't seem to have."

"Yeah? What's that?"

"You *can* change. You just need some help."

He looked at her bleakly. "You really *don't* understand. Who'd help *me* change, Lexi?" His lip twisted. "My dad? All he can think about is his new wife and baby. My mom? She's hundreds of miles away trying to make a new life for herself. Teachers? They'd rather see me in reform school than at Cedar River High. Who'd help me, Lexi?" His voice rose on a plaintive note.

"God would."

"Ah hah! This is where the religious stuff comes in!" His dark eyes narrowed and his finely chiseled jaw tightened, but this time Lexi was unafraid.

"This is where the *power* comes in."

"Power?" he mimicked.

"Sure. The power of God. The main source of all power. Tap into that and you can be the person you're meant to be. The trouble is, without His power you're exactly right: you *can't* change."

"This holy electrical generator stuff is fascinating, Lexi," Matt sneered, "but it's not for me. I'm on the school administration's 'watch closely' list. If anything goes wrong, I'm the first one pulled into the office. Even if I wanted to change now—which I don't—nobody would let me."

"Don't let that get you down. You can change, and if you do—really change, I mean—then they'll have to believe you. Don't condemn yourself, and don't let others do it either." She leaned forward for emphasis as she spoke.

"Nice pep talk, Lexi. Too bad I don't believe it."

"There's a verse from the Bible that my dad likes to quote sometimes," Lexi offered. "It's Luke 4:18 and talks about Jesus healing the brokenhearted and binding up their wounds. Seems to me you could use someone to do that for you."

"I'm not brokenhearted," Matt snorted.

"Aren't you? Even when you think about your mom and sister—"

"Don't talk about them!" He bolted off the seat. "Don't remind me about them! They're gone. There's nothing I can do . . ." His voice trailed away.

Matt glanced down at his wristwatch and a flicker of relief lit his eyes. "My half hour is up. I've gotta go. And I won't say it's been nice talking to you, Lexi, because it hasn't." He stared at her until she felt like squirming. "You're the most *uncomfortable* person I've ever met."

Lexi blinked with surprise. "I'm not uncomfortable, Matt. I feel fine."

"No?" A little grin twisted at the corner of his lip. "But *I'm* uncomfortable." His voice softened. "Listen, Lexi, I appreciate what you're trying to do, but I don't want to change. I want to stay mad, because everything hurts less when you're mad. And I don't want people close to me, Lexi. I want them scared. Understand?"

Lexi nodded. "But I still want you to think about what I said."

Matt gave a little groan of frustration. "Put a lid on it, Lexi. Please?" He pivoted on his toe and started off toward the nursing home at a slow lope. When Ben waved at him from the swings, Matt lifted a hand in acknowledgment.

Thoughtfully Lexi drew her knees to her chest and wrapped her arms around her legs. She'd been studying about the war between the states in history class. North against South, father against son, brother against brother. That's what Matt reminded her of right now—someone fighting against himself and the battleground was his heart. If he didn't stop pulling himself in so many directions, he was going to tear himself apart.

Jennifer was lounged across the front steps when Ben and Lexi arrived at home from the park.

"What are you doing here?" Lexi asked. "I thought you had studying to do."

"I do. I can only take so much before my brain rebels. Want to call Binky and Peggy and see if they want to play some doubles? I brought my tennis racket."

"Binky is baby-sitting today," Lexi said. "And Peggy—"

"I know, I know, she's with Chad." Jennifer made a face. "This is getting totally out of hand. You can't even talk to Peggy alone anymore. If they get any closer, they're going to have to be separated surgically!"

"Come on inside," Lexi invited, ignoring her friend's speculation about Peggy. "I want to show you the photos I took for the paper. They're pretty good, I think."

Jennifer stretched and stood up. "Since you've been on staff the paper has improved about three million percent."

"That good?"

"You know what I mean. Now if they'd only yank Minda off the staff—"

"Don't you like her columns?"

"Not really." Jennifer gave a careless shrug. "Minda thinks she's so fashion conscious, but *you're* the one who studies all the magazines and sews whatever you want. You'd be a better choice for that column."

"Thanks but no thanks." Lexi shuddered. "I can't think of a better way to get more firmly entrenched on Minda's hate list than to offer to take over her column!" She spread the black and white photos on the dining room table as they talked.

"I suppose so. Anyway, it's not the fashion column that bothers me. It's the gossip column she does every other issue that drives me crazy." Jennifer mimicked, " 'Who's the blond that chopped her hair off at the roots for a little attention? Tell me, do balds really have more fun?' "

"Ignore it. She was trying to get to you."

"Well, she did a good job."

Lexi smiled. "Actually, the column can be pretty funny—if you aren't in it."

"True. Minda is creative. Too bad she spends her time devouring unsuspecting humans instead of doing something productive." Jennifer sorted through the photos on the table. "Here's a good one of Matt Windsor. You should probably give that one to Minda. He hasn't had any exposure in her column yet."

"I doubt that he will," Lexi murmured.

"No? Not until Minda finds someone else she considers more 'interesting.' Just wait and see."

Perhaps Jennifer was right. Anyone who crossed Minda or displeased her in any way usually ended up being embarrassed in the column. Lexi was waiting for her own turn. No doubt Minda had something particularly onerous waiting for her. Maybe even the suspense of waiting was punishment enough.

The only reason Mrs. Drummond had allowed the column to print was that it was really very witty and well written. Minda had assured the teacher that everything was in "good fun" and that the students didn't seem to mind being poked fun at in the paper.

Minda's assertions had been supported by a flood of fan mail in the paper's suggestion box. Lexi suspected that the Hi-Five members were the ones writing, but apparently that thought hadn't occurred to Mrs. Drummond, and the column ran.

Thinking about Minda was just as frustrating as thinking about Matt, Lexi decided. And today she didn't feel like being frustrated.

"Want to stay for supper?" she asked Jennifer.

"That depends. Are you having liver?"

"I don't think so."

"Beets or broccoli?"

"Very doubtful."

"Spinach?"

"Definitely not."

"Good. Then I'll stay."

Laughing, the pair made their way to the kitchen.

Chapter Nine

"Where are you going in such a hurry?" Todd wondered as Lexi threw school books into her locker and pulled out her jacket. "Is this a fire drill?" He leaned against the bank of lockers next to her, looking as though he had all the time in the world.

"We had to stay overtime in my last class." Lexi scanned the nearly deserted hallways. "Some idiot glued the pages of Mr. Johnson's lesson planner together and—"

"Until somebody 'fessed up everyone had to stay," Todd concluded.

"Some of them are still sitting in the classroom. The glue was still damp, so it had to have been done the previous hour. Those of us who had class that period finally got to leave."

"The mystery deepens." Todd wiggled his eyebrows. "You still didn't tell me why you're in such a hurry."

"It's Ben." Lexi tugged at the spiral notebook that had become stuck on the slats of her locker. "Mom had a dental appointment this afternoon. She didn't want to take Ben because he hates the sounds and

84

smells and gets panicky. Rather than get a babysitter, she said she'd have him wait for me outside the door of the high school. I told her that if I wasn't there she should just leave. I'd planned to be early and I'm nearly fifteen minutes late!"

"Calm down," Todd said soothingly. "Give me your books. Ben will be fine."

"You know how Ben is," Lexi muttered. "If he decides to wander off—"

"He won't. He knows what can happen now. He'll stay put."

Lexi looked doubtfully at Todd. She wished she could believe him. Every time Ben was left alone he managed to get into some sort of trouble—lost, hit by a car. . . . Lexi left the notebook dangling from the locker door and started to run. Todd pulled the notebook free and hurried after her.

"If he's not there, I'll—" The words froze on her lips as she started out the wide double doors of the high school.

Ben was there all right, sitting obediently on the bench where his mother had placed him. His schoolbag was over his knees and he clutched at the handle until his knuckles were white with exertion. His almond-shaped eyes were wide and his mouth puckered with interest. Surrounding him were five rough looking young men.

"Who are *they*?" Lexi asked.

When Todd didn't answer, she turned to look at him and gave a small gasp. "Todd! What's wrong?"

"Those guys." His eyes grew narrow and watchful. "Matt Windsor hangs out with them sometimes. Seems to me they look a little too interested in Ben."

Just then one of the scraggly haired youths poked

at Ben with the toe of his scuffed leather boot. Ben squirmed away only to bump into another who had taken a seat beside him.

Lexi took a step to move through the door but Todd stopped her. "Wait."

"I can't wait! Those thugs could beat up on—"

She glanced toward Ben only to see Matt sauntering slowly toward the group.

"Let Matt do it," Todd whispered. With his arm firmly around her shoulder, he guided her through the door to where they couldn't be observed. "Just watch."

"Look what we found, Windsor! A kid." The boy on the bench yelled. Then he turned to Ben. "Want to share your bag with us, kid?" Ben clutched even more tightly to his bag. Lexi struggled to get out of Todd's grasp.

She could see that even Ben, who considered everyone his friend, was getting scared. No one he knew ever talked to him that way—in such a mocking, derisive tone.

"Let Matt handle it, Lexi," Todd told her again. "Otherwise Ben might get hurt."

She looked doubtfully at Matt's black leather back. What if he didn't realize how frightened Ben was? What if he didn't have any compassion for a little boy who didn't understand when people were making fun of him? Todd certainly had a lot more confidence in Matt than she did.

"Leave the kid alone, Frankie," Matt ordered nonchalantly.

"Why? Maybe I want to see what's so special about this bag of his." He poked at Ben's schoolbag, and Ben's lower lip began to tremble.

"You taking up baby-sitting?" Matt inquired sharply.

"What-sa-matter, Windsor? You going soft on us? Feeling sorry for this little punk?"

Matt shrugged. "Hey, what do you think?" He sauntered a little closer.

Lexi held her breath. Poor Ben looked terrified. Then his chin came up and a flicker of something other than fear seemed to enter his eyes.

"Hi, Matt," Ben said, his voice clear and strong.

"You know this kid, Matt?" one of the young men asked. "Maybe it's *you* that's taken up baby-sitting."

The way Lexi saw it, Matt had two choices. He could admit that he did know Ben and tell them to leave the little boy alone or he could save face—no matter what the cost to Ben.

"I'm going out there," she announced. "Matt won't help him!" She struggled in Todd's grasp. "Let go of me."

"Give him a chance, Lexi. Matt won't let Ben get hurt." Todd's grip tightened on her shoulder.

Todd understood something about Matt that she did not. As Lexi watched, Matt held out his hand to Ben.

Ben scrambled down off the bench and trustingly put his hand into Matt's. "Where's Lexi?"

"I don't know. We'll go find her, okay?"

Ben's head bobbed happily. "Find Lexi." He tipped his face toward Matt and gave him a sweet smile.

It took a moment for the others to grasp what Matt was doing.

"Windsor!" Frankie hooted. "My ma needs a baby-sitter for tonight. Are you free?"

"I hear the nursery school down the street needs some part-time help. Maybe you could apply."

The taunts followed Matt and Ben as they walked toward the school. When they reached the bottom step, Lexi bolted through the doorway and scooped Ben into her arms.

"Lexi lost?" Ben wondered as he brushed the palms of his hands against her cheeks and gave her a happy smile.

"Just a little late, Punkin. So sorry."

When Lexi stood up, Matt was glaring at her. "You shouldn't have left him there. He could have gotten hurt."

Lexi blinked. This was a switch! Matt Windsor scolding *her* for something. "I know, Matt. We got held after class and . . ." She spread her hands in a gesture of frustration.

"Ah? Well, don't let it happen again." Roughly he tousled the top of Ben's silky head and turned away.

"Matt?"

"What?" Impatiently he turned back to her.

"Todd and I were watching through the door. Thanks for standing up for Ben. We heard what those guys said. I know they'll give you a hard time about being an easy touch."

"Oh, ah?" He tossed back his head and his dark hair glinted. "Well, the total IQ of those five guys doesn't add up to my shoe size." Then a grin split his features. "And I don't wear very big shoes."

At that, he turned and walked away, his swaggering saunter just a little more pronounced than usual.

Lexi breathed a gusty sigh of relief. "You were right, Todd. He did watch out for Ben."

"Matt's all right. I know he is. That tough stuff is just an act, Lexi. The Matt you saw today is the real Matt—the old Matt." Todd ran his fingers through his hair. "Sometimes I think that Matt doesn't even like himself anymore."

Lexi was quiet so long that Todd finally gave her elbow a little shake.

"Are you still with me?"

"Ah." She rubbed her fingers across her eyes. "I was just wishing that Matt would see what he's doing to himself. Do you think it's possible that he ever will?"

Todd shrugged. "Maybe, maybe not. It's going to take something big to change him now."

———

"Are you going to Gina William's party?" Binky wondered aloud as Lexi met her at the school door.

Lexi glanced at Binky. "I don't know. How about you?"

Binky shrugged. "Only if the rest of you go. Chad and Peggy will be off in some corner making fools of themselves and Egg will be following Minda around like he's chained to her. What fun will I have if there's no one to talk to?"

"There'll be a whole room full of people, Binky!"

Binky's petite features crumbled. "Nobody like you guys. Tressa's group isn't exactly known for being friendly."

Gina, a member of Hi-Five, was also on the newspaper staff. She'd invited everyone from the newspaper and the yearbook staff as well as her usual group to a party at her home.

"Anyway, what will I talk about? The only reason

I was invited was because Egg is on the paper staff and they knew he wouldn't leave me behind."

"Great confidence you have, Binky," Lexi chastised softly. "Maybe Gina invited you because she *wanted* you there."

Binky cast her a doubtful glance. "You and I both know better, Lexi, but thanks anyway."

Poor Binky, Lexi thought to herself. Her self-confidence took a nose-dive whenever any of the Hi-Fives were around.

"Tell you what, Todd and I will pick you and Egg up around seven."

"Do you mind? It would be great if—"

"Of course not. Be ready at seven."

———

By 7:20 Lexi understood Binky's hesitation to come to the party.

The Williamses' home was a six-bedroom sprawling ranch style house in a pseudo-Spanish motif on the edge of Cedar River. Lexi had never seen such a large foyer. The flooring was quarry tile, the interior walls stucco, the light fixtures wrought iron. It led in one direction to a massive dark oak kitchen, in another to a formal living room filled with massive Spanish-looking furniture, and in a third to a family room.

The buzz of voices was already escalating. Several boys were clustered around a bank of pinball machines, while others were involved in stuffing a Nerf basketball through a hoop suspended from a light fixture. At the far end of the room was a bar.

"Got anything in there stronger than this?" someone was asking.

Tressa, Gina's sister, seemed to be in charge and gave a tight smile. "Sorry. Dad locked it up and took the key."

"Awwwhhhh! What's he trying to do? Ruin the party?"

Lexi and Todd exchanged glances.

"Smart dad," Todd whispered. "These guys would pull this place apart if they could get into the liquor cabinet."

"Her parents aren't here?" Lexi wondered. Her own mother and father would never consider leaving the house if she were having a party. They were good about staying discreetly out of the way, but not for a moment would they leave the house.

Todd shook his head. "I doubt it. The Williamses travel a lot. They might not even be in the country."

Lexi squirmed uncomfortably at that thought. Already the party was more rowdy than any she'd ever been to and the evening was still young.

"Come on, let's go find something to eat," Todd suggested. He led the way to the kitchen where still another group mingled. The table was piled high with chips and dip, caramel corn and fudge brownies.

"All right! This is what I was looking for!"

As Todd helped himself to food, Lexi glanced around. This wasn't just the newspaper and yearbook staff, she realized. Most of the high school seemed to be here—and a few she didn't recognize.

Suddenly, she drew a sharp breath. Across the room, lounging lazily against a china cabinet full of dishes, was one of the boys who'd been tormenting Ben.

"Todd." She pulled on his sleeve. "Those are the guys who—"

"I know. The ones who were teasing Ben. Matt hangs out with them a lot. He must be here too."

Of course. Tressa and Minda were friends, and Minda was crazy about Matt. It was perfectly clear why those tough boys were invited—to insure Matt's presence at the party.

They returned to the living room where they found Binky and Jennifer in deep discussion with two boys from their math class. Lexi smiled to herself. Binky seemed to be doing just fine without their company. Her eyes were sparkling and she laughed occasionally at some anecdote.

Poor Egg, Lexi observed. He was having a tough time keeping up with Minda tonight. She flitted from place to place, acting as though she were the hostess of the party, instead of Tressa. Lexi had a hunch that she would soon flit to the kitchen in search of Matt.

"Well, what do you think?" Todd inquired. He'd finally set down his plate after packing away a half dozen brownies and most of a bag of chips.

"The parties in Grover's Point were never like this."

He chuckled. "Most of the parties in Cedar River aren't either." He glanced around. "In fact, this is getting a little wild even for a Tressa Williams get-together."

It seemed that since Mr. Williams' liquor cabinet was off limits, someone had gone out and found their own. Two boys were passing out beer cans at the far end of the family room.

"I think I'd like to go, Todd," Lexi murmured. "I really don't feel comfortable."

He nodded obligingly. "Okay. What about Egg and Binky?"

"I'll find them. If they want to stay, maybe they can get a ride with someone else." Lexi stood up and brushed the front of her wool slacks. "I suppose I'm a real dud, but . . ." She knew what her parents would say if they saw this place.

"You don't have to explain to me," Todd reminded her. "Go find Binky." She gave Todd a grateful glance. At least there was one person here on her wavelength.

Binky was no longer in the living room. Neither was she in the kitchen or the family room. Lexi checked three bathrooms and the laundry room before she heard voices in the back bedroom.

How did Binky ever manage to get back here? Lexi wondered. Apparently none of the house was off-limits to the partygoers. She knocked softly on the door.

"Who is it?"

"It's me—Lexi. Is Binky in there?"

"Who?"

"Binky McNaughton, I—"

"Come in, I can't hear you!"

Lexi pushed open the door.

Surely this must be Tressa's bedroom. It was pale blue and peach from the ceiling to the floor. A floral blue and peach spread covered the bed, and Minda Hannaford lay sprawled on top of it.

Lexi's first notion was that Minda was sick.

"Minda, are you okay?"

Minda was propped against the frothy pillows, her blond hair a cloud of gold around her face. Tressa was in an overstuffed chair next to the bed.

The scene struck Lexi as a little odd, but she didn't question it. Not, that is, until she smelled the sickly sweet scent of incense—or something else.

"What are you doing?" Lexi blurted.

Minda gave her an innocent stare. Then she picked up the stubby, self-rolled cigarette that had been in the ashtray and took a deep, inhaling drag.

"Just having a smoke, that's all."

"That's not 'just' a smoke, Minda. That's—"

"My, my! The girl isn't as naive as we thought! She recognizes a joint when she sees one!" Minda announced happily. Her head dipped and bobbed a little as she spoke. "I'm going to have to rethink my feelings about you, Lexi." Then her eyes narrowed. "Of course, if you're going to get me all upset by talking religion, I'll have to hate you. You *do* realize that, don't you?" She smiled benignly. "I don't want this great party, and my reputation, ruined by *your* religion."

Lexi felt a sick knot in her stomach. What possessed Minda to do these things?

Minda answered the question herself.

"You haven't seen Matt out there, have you? I was wondering if he'd like to come in and join me." Her eyes fluttered coyly. "He is so *cute*."

A ploy to impress Matt—and a stupid one, at that.

"I don't think you should be—" Lexi began.

"Don't lecture, Lexi. You're boring when you lecture." Minda squirmed to the side of the bed. "And I hate boring people."

Just then, as Minda took another deep drag on the diminishing joint, Lexi felt a presence behind her. Todd?

She turned and a little gasp of surprise escaped her. It was Matt.

"Todd is looking for you, Lexi. He found Binky outside playing horseshoes and . . . what are you doing?" His eyes were riveted on Minda.

She gave him a relaxed, lopsided smile as she patted the edge of the bed. "Come and join me, Matt. Have a smoke."

Matt strode across the room in three swift steps. His hand was on the joint, grinding it into the ashtray before Minda could protest.

"What do you think you're doing?" she yelped. "Stop that!"

"No, *you* stop it. That stuff is no good for you."

She gave him an angry, indignant stare. "Then why do you smoke it?"

Matt opened his mouth to answer and then closed it again. Finally he blurted. "It's none of your business."

Minda was still too much under the influence of the marijuana to be afraid. "Sure it's my business! Why do you think I tried it in the first place?" She pointed an accusing finger at Matt. "Because of you!"

"Me?" The word came out in a strangled tone.

"Of course." Minda waved her arms like a floppy rag doll as Lexi stared. "How else could I impress you? You never even noticed my existence . . ." she giggled ". . . until now."

With a pained expression on his face, Matt abruptly turned on his heel and walked out.

Rather than watch the surprised, then defeated expression on Minda's face, Lexi followed Matt into the hallway.

When she caught up to him, he was standing at

the end of the hall by a window, staring out into the evening darkness.

"Matt?" she ventured. He looked miserable standing there, but even Lexi wasn't prepared for the anguish in his eyes when he turned around.

Chapter Ten

"I found Binky outside. She was . . ." Todd began as he sauntered up to the pair in the hallway. Then his voice took on a sharp note of concern. "What's going on?"

Lexi grimaced. "I found something I wasn't looking for—Minda—smoking a joint."

Todd's eyebrows arched. "Really? I thought Minda was too smart for that sort of thing." He motioned toward Matt who stood pillarlike near the window, a question in his eyes.

Lexi shrugged her shoulders. His behavior was as puzzling to her as it was to Todd.

"Matt?" Todd finally ventured.

Matt spun around and abruptly announced, "I'm getting out of here."

"Want to come with us?" Todd offered. "Or do you have your bike?"

Matt shook his head. "I need a ride. Come on, let's go."

"What about Binky and—" Lexi began.

"They're going to leave with Peggy and Chad." Todd took her elbow and steered her toward the door.

Silently, the odd threesome trooped through the house and out to Todd's 1949 Ford Coupe. Matt flung himself into the back.

After thirty silent minutes in which Todd drove aimlessly about town, Matt leaned forward over the front seat.

"You can take me home."

"How about something to eat first?" Todd offered. "I could use a burger."

"Okay." Matt sank back into the velvety cushions of the old car.

Silently they pulled into the parking lot of the Hamburger Shack.

It was nearly closing time. The back booths had already been cleaned and a few tables had chairs tipped upside down on top of them, but the waitress took their order and they seated themselves in the front booth. The blinking neon light outside the building flashed a glow of orange and pink across their table.

Lexi was becoming uncomfortable. Todd seemed to understand Matt and his need for silence, but it made her squirm. She was a doer, and waiting for something to happen was hard on Lexi.

It surprised her, however, that when Matt spoke, it was to her.

"Do you think she meant it?"

Lexi blinked. "Who? Meant what?"

"Minda. About smoking pot because of me."

Lexi considered the question. "I don't know. I *do* know that she's got a big crush on you, but . . ." and she paused thoughtfully, "I really don't think Minda does anything for anyone but herself."

Todd nodded. "Minda does what Minda wants."

"But what she *wanted* was to impress me." Matt seemed both perturbed and puzzled by the fact. He was silent a long time and when he spoke his voice was small, almost childlike.

"I never meant for this to happen."

"For what to happen?" Todd asked softly.

"This. Everything. My life. All of it." He gestured at his jacket, his hair, the single earring in his ear. Matt looked around with an angry expression. "I suppose I meant to hurt my dad," he admitted finally. "And especially my stepmother. I *wanted* them to know that when my mom went away and they got married, it ruined my life." He paused. "But I didn't mean for others to do stupid things because they thought it would please me."

"Like Minda?"

"Yeah. Drugs are dumb. I know that. But it doesn't matter if I get hurt. I just don't want to be responsible if others . . ." His voice trailed away.

"It does so matter! You matter!" Lexi pounded her fist hard against the table. "Don't talk like that!"

Matt gave her a pitying look. "You don't understand, do you? What have I got? A mother and a sister I never see. A father who's crazy about a woman closer to my age than to his. A pregnant stepmother who's already worrying about keeping me and her baby apart so I don't hurt it. Why should I care what happens to me?"

His words tore a jagged thrust of pain through Lexi, and a response flowed freely from her lips.

"I care! Todd cares! Even Minda cares or she wouldn't be trying so hard to impress you!" Impulsively she leaned across the table and took Matt's hand in her own. It was icy cold. "God cares."

He drew his hand away so quickly Lexi hardly realized what had happened. "Don't talk about God."

"But He does care! Even if you won't let me talk about it, it's happening!"

"No." His voice was flat and final.

"What makes you so sure?"

"Nobody, not even God, will forgive the kind of stuff I've done."

"Oh?" Todd interjected, his voice mocking. "You mean you're worse than everybody else? Everybody who ever existed?"

Matt gave him a don't-be-stupid look.

"And because you're so bad, He won't forgive you?"

"Something like that." Matt shoved himself away from the table. "I've gotta go. Thanks for the ride and—"

Their order arrived just as Matt made his attempt to stand. Blocked in by the waitress, he sank back to his seat.

"You might as well eat," Todd observed calmly, sprinkling salt across his plate of fries. "Unless, of course, you think sitting across from you will make us sick."

Anger flared in Matt's eyes. "What is that supposed to mean?"

"It means that since you're so good at deciding things for others, I thought maybe you'd decided that too."

Matt's shoulders slumped. "Knock it off, Todd."

Coolly, Todd retorted, "No, *you* knock it off. Quit deciding what other people think of you. And especially quit deciding what God thinks of you. You haven't got one clue about the way His mind works. I can see that already."

"And you guys do?" Matt sneered. "How'd you hook into *that* pipeline?" Calmly Lexi lifted a New Testament out of her purse. "Through this."

Matt glanced at the book lying on the table and looked away. "Written especially for you, I suppose."

Todd and Lexi's voices chimed together, "Yes."

Matt stared at them in disbelief.

Lexi flicked open the book. "And you too. You just don't know it yet."

Matt snorted. "How do you expect me to believe that? Especially coming from Little Miss Perfect and her boyfriend."

"We aren't perfect. It says so right here." Lexi pointed to Rom. 3:23 and Matt read it out loud.

" 'All have sinned and fall short of the glory of God. . . .' So? What's that supposed to mean?"

"It means that we are all in the same boat. *None* of us is living up to God's expectations."

"I don't believe that." Matt frowned. "What are you two doing wrong?"

"I can assure you, we aren't perfect, Matt. And to a God who is perfect all sins are equally awful."

"Great. I feel much better. Now I know that you guys are in as deep a trouble as me," Matt sneered.

"But God also gave us a way out of all this," Todd insisted urgently.

"I should have known! A secret passage! A hidden tunnel! You've been reading too many dumb mysteries, Lexi."

She smiled serenely and quoted from 1 John 1:9: " 'If we confess our sins, he [God] is faithful and just to forgive us our sins and to cleanse us from all un-righteousness.' "

"Huh?"

"It means that if we're sorry for what we've done wrong and confess it to God, He'll forgive us."

"Just like that?" Matt snapped his fingers. He looked from Lexi to Todd and back again.

"Just like that."

"So what do you have to do first?"

"Nothing. Just believe Him."

"I don't get it. Sounds too easy."

Lexi smiled. "Believing isn't always easy, Matt. All the doubts you have keep moving in. You just have to claim God's promise and hang on to the fact that He never lies."

"Never?"

"Never."

Matt gave another doubtful scowl. He poked his finger at the little Testament on the table. "Can I borrow that?"

"Sure. You can have it," Lexi offered.

"Don't you need it?"

"I've got another at home."

Matt fingered the book for a moment; then it disappeared inside his jacket. Abruptly, he stood. "*Now* I want to go."

Agreeably, Todd and Lexi nodded. It was definitely time to go home. God had already accomplished the impossible. Matt Winsdor was carrying a Bible in his front pocket.

Chapter Eleven

Whatever Matt had read over the weekend had an impact, Lexi decided as she watched him saunter down the hall on Monday morning. Everything about him seemed a little more relaxed, a little . . . softer.

The black jacket was still in place, as was the strange haircut, but—and it took Lexi a moment to figure out what the difference was—instead of black boots Matt was wearing tennis shoes.

Rather than ignore her as he usually did, Matt stopped and began to talk.

"You know that book you gave me?"

Lexi nodded.

"I was just wondering if there was"—his features flushed—"more."

"More?"

"Yeah. More chapters or whatever they're called. It's pretty interesting."

"That was the New Testament. There's an Old Testament as well, which tells the history of the Jews and goes up until the time of Christ."

"Okay. I want that too."

It took all her willpower not to giggle. She'd never

seen Matt so excited. "Why don't you come home with me after school. We have dozens of Bibles around the house. I'll give you one."

"Give it to me? Just like that?" His eyes widened.

"Sure. Why not?"

"But don't you need it?"

"Of course. But we have others." She paused before adding, "I have a hunch this will be your only one."

Matt Windsor's metamorphosis had begun.

First it was the shoes. Then the haircut, which he had trimmed to a little less outlandish shape. Then the skin-tight denim jeans were occasionally replaced by corduroys.

But the most noticeable change of all was his smile.

"He must be up to something," Egg deduced one day upon exiting a class he had with Matt. "He laughed out loud in class. Scared us all! We thought maybe he'd planted a bomb in the room and was just waiting for it to go off!"

"Give the guy a little credit, Egg," Lexi chided. "You like to laugh. Maybe Matt does too."

Egg looked doubtful. "It's not like him, Lexi. Something funny is going on."

Lexi was hard-pressed to remain silent. The "something funny" was Matt's discovery of the good news of the Gospel.

Both she and Todd had been feeding him books from their families' personal libraries at a rate that astounded them both. He'd read everything he could find on forgiveness, then prayer. Matt was like a dry sponge touching water for the first time.

And the questions!

The three of them had begun to meet at Lexi's house after school to discuss what Matt had read the night before. Lexi was amazed at the quickness of Matt's mind. Soon her mother and father had begun to join them in an attempt to answer all of Matt's questions.

One evening, when Mr. and Mrs. Leighton were attending a banquet and Ben was playing quietly in his room, Matt dropped a bombshell.

"You know," he began, "the way I figure it, I'm going to have to do something about my parents pretty soon."

"Do what?"

"I don't exactly know. They're so used to me being not home or in my room that I don't think they realize what's been happening to me." His eyes clouded. "I've decided that I have to accept my stepmother. I read somewhere in Ephesians that you should 'honor your father and your mother.' She is my mother now." His eyes flickered. "But I don't like it."

"What will you do?" Lexi wondered. It was difficult to imagine how hard this all must be on Matt.

"Try to apologize, I guess. Maybe if I offer to give them another chance, they'll give me one too." He looked uncharacteristically unsure of himself. "Do you think it will work?"

"Have you prayed about it?"

Matt frowned. "I think so. At least I tried. It feels pretty . . . strange."

"Maybe we could pray too—Todd and I," Lexi offered. "A little help never hurts."

"You'd do that?"

"Of course." Lexi's expression softened. "It's called intercessory prayer, Matt. That's when people pray for one another's needs. If one prayer can unleash God's power, just think how much can be accomplished with many people praying."

Matt thought about it for a second and then asked the question that Todd and Lexi were beginning to expect from him. "Have you got a book about it?"

Todd burst out laughing. "When do you find time for schoolwork, Matt?"

Matt grinned wickedly. "Who says I'm doing any schoolwork?" Then his expression turned somber. "I'm going to talk to my folks on Saturday. Remember now," and he pointed a warning finger between the two of them, "you promised to pray."

———

Lexi didn't see much of Matt in the following days. Still, each night Matt was at the top of her prayer list.

Todd brought word on Wednesday that the Emerald Tones were planning to hold open tryouts. The Emerald Tones was an elite group of Cedar River's best singers. Only one-tenth of the students who tried out were asked to join the group.

Tryouts were forgotten however, when a big flurry erupted over Minda's most recent column in the school newspaper.

"How dare she say that?" Peggy fumed, her cheeks a bright, unhealthy pink. "How dare she make fun of Chad and me in the school newspaper!"

Lexi and Jennifer had been trying to calm Peggy down for some moments, but she insisted on pacing

Jennifer's bedroom floor, waving her arms and muttering about Minda Hannaford.

Lexi had a piercing pain in her head. The uproar had been escalating all day. She picked up a copy of the paper and flipped to Minda's column.

Minda had resorted to a type of scandal-sheet patter for her format. It was breezy, interesting—and highly embarrassing to the target of her attacks.

"Who says blonds have more fun?" read one line. "Take a look at the brunettes who've discovered a peephole into the men's locker room!"

Lexi grinned. That was rather funny, actually. Especially considering that everyone in school knew the peephole viewed only the entrance and exit to the locker room and not any part of the shower area. Still, it caused the administration to send every janitor in the building down to the locker room to patch cracks and examine the walls.

"Has anyone told the school cooks that salmon loaf is dangerous to the health?" read another item. "It causes students to swim upstream, trying to get away from the cafeteria."

Then her eyes fell on the line that was causing Peggy so much dismay.

"Who is the couple making absolute fools of themselves in the hallways of Cedar River High? Can't they see it's no place for romance? Save the cuddling for private, folks!"

Of course, there was no mention of names or places, but Peggy and Chad were likely candidates for the dubious honor of appearing in Minda's column. Lexi thought back to the difficult time she'd had talking to Peggy about her romance with Chad.

"Forget it, Peggy," Jennifer advised. "If you pretend you don't know who Minda is talking about, it will blow over. If you make a big deal of it, you're going to show up in her next column too."

Lexi nodded in agreement.

"But I'm so embarrassed!" Peggy wailed. "The guys have been teasing Chad and—"

"Then why don't you quit holding hands and kissing each other goodbye between classes," Lexi recommended softly.

The room grew so quiet Lexi could hear the quiet purr of Jennifer's electric alarm clock.

After a long moment, Peggy sprang into action. "I have to go now. I don't think I have anything more to say here." With that, she gathered up her books from the corner of the bed and walked out the door, head held high.

Jennifer whistled through her teeth. "Boy, did you make her mad."

"I didn't mean to," Lexi murmured.

"Are you going to say you're sorry?"

"I'm not sorry. Peggy and Chad *have* been acting silly. They embarrass me and they embarrass themselves."

"True," Jennifer agreed. "But she's your friend."

"I know. And sometimes friends have to say things that others don't like to hear."

Jennifer shook her head. "You've got guts, Lexi. I can say that much for you."

Chapter Twelve

Though Peggy had nearly quit speaking to Lexi over the item in Minda's column, Minda was blissfully unaware of the trouble she'd caused. She had quickly found other things to cover.

Those "other things" included the gradual, yet obvious changes in Matt Windsor. One afternoon, after the Emerald Tones had finished practicing, Lexi came upon Minda holding court in the newspaper room complaining loudly and verbally about the changes she had noticed in Matt.

"What's wrong with him these days?" she wondered aloud to several of the Hi-Fives who were gathered around. "He used to be so totally rad and now he's so . . . ordinary."

Matt? Ordinary? Lexi wondered to herself. Even though he'd slowly shed some of the outer trappings that made him look so fierce, Matt was still far from ordinary. His hair had grown out now and was cut in a style not unlike Todd's. Shorter on the sides and top, slightly longer in the back and just like ninety-nine percent of the boys who attended Cedar River.

The black leather jacket was still in place, but

now it covered an array of corduroys, denims, and plaid shirts—even a preppy buttoned-down shirt or two instead of the plain black T-shirts with a skull and cross-bones emblazoned upon them. The black boots seemed to have vanished completely in favor of slip-on shoes or his good old standby, the laceless, high-top tennis shoes.

Matt no longer stood out in the crowd unless he chose to by straightening his shoulders, giving his head a defiant toss and moving into a graceful swagger that Lexi had so often noticed.

"He's absolutely boring!" Minda insisted aloud.

"I don't know," Tressa piped up. "I think he's cute!"

"Cute!" Minda snorted. "Maybe, if you like that type." She said "type" disparagingly as if the person Matt was becoming had stepped off the pages of a Sears catalog rather than that of a Harley-Davidson cycle magazine.

Lexi smiled to herself. If only you knew, Minda, just how *much* Matt has changed! He was quiet about his activities around school, but Matt had been coming to a small Bible study that Mr. and Mrs. Leighton sponsored in their home on Sunday evenings. Though most of the group were adults, Matt's quick mind and his eagerness had charmed them all and they found themselves learning in response to his questions.

"He's just no fun anymore," Minda complained. "I mean, really, what's the point?"

Lexi knew exactly what the "point" was. Perhaps she hadn't consciously realized it, but Minda had been using Matt as a tool for her own rebellion. Minda's home life was not a happy one. Hanging around with bad-boy Matt was just one more way to force her parents to pay attention to her rather than their own troubles of alcohol and divorce.

"Just lay off Matt," someone declared. "He's all right. I like him better this way. He talked to me in the hallway yesterday and he's never done that before."

Minda gave a delicate sniff. "Well, well, he's even gotten sociable now, has he?" Her eyes narrowed. "I think it's time for Matt Windsor to realize just how boring he's become."

"Now, Minda," Tressa warned. "Don't go and do anything foolish—"

"Me? Do something foolish?" Minda battered her long lustrous eyelashes coyly. "Why, Tressa, have you ever known me to do anything foolish?"

Lexi groaned inwardly. She'd only lived in Cedar River a couple of months, and she alone could make a list of fifteen or twenty foolish things Minda had managed to do in that brief amount of time. Before she could dwell on the dark possibilities, Mrs. Drummond hurried into the room, clapping her hands and announcing, "All right, everyone. We have to get moving on the paper. The administration would like us to put out an extra edition somewhere during the year, and I think now is as good a time as any. Lexi, do you and Todd have any photos that could be used for this issue?"

Lexi nodded. "We just took several pictures of the Emerald Tones," she explained. "Since Mrs. Waverly is considering arranging a tour, we thought it might be a good idea to have a layout on them in the paper."

"Very good," Mrs. Drummond smiled. "I always know I can count on you and Todd to come up with something creative. Any other ideas, anyone?" she asked, glancing around the room. Minda's hand shot into the air.

"What kind of a column do you want me to do? Fashion? Or another chitchat column?"

Mrs. Drummond paused. "Well, we did have your fashion column in the last paper, Minda, but, considering the fact there have been some complaints about the 'gossip' column you've written, perhaps we should—"

"Complaints mean they're reading the column, Mrs. Drummond." Minda wore her most endearing, conniving, look. "Why don't you give me one more chance?"

Mrs. Drummond hesitated. The newspaper's comment box *had* been jammed full of complaints and praise concerning Minda's last column. After all, wasn't that part of what this was all about? Getting students to read other students' work? Lexi could practically guess Mrs. Drummond's thoughts. She could see the teacher weakening.

"Then just be a little more careful this time with your column, Minda. Remember, the idea is to be chatty and informative, not nasty—intentionally or otherwise."

Minda batted her long eyelashes over big blue eyes and looked as innocent as a newborn babe. "I never intend to be nasty, Mrs. Drummond. Sometimes people just take it that way."

Mrs. Drummond cast her a doubtful glance. "Very well, then. You do your chitchat column and Tressa, I'd like you to write a feature on. . . ."

Lexi didn't like the expression on Minda's features one bit. She looked so pleased and self-satisfied that if she were a cat, Lexi had no doubt she would be burping up the family canary. Then Lexi felt a wave of guilt. Maybe she was underestimating Minda. Maybe the girl didn't have an ulterior motive for every single thing she did. Maybe it only *seemed* that way.

———

"Is she talking to you yet?" Jennifer wondered idly as she swirled long strands of spaghetti around on her nearly empty plate.

"Peggy, you mean?" Lexi sighed.

"Who else?"

"No, not exactly. We say 'hello' in the hallways and sometimes we sit at the same table for lunch, but she never waits for me to walk to school with her anymore. Every time she looks at me, she has this hurt expression in her eyes." Lexi swirled a noodle onto her fork. "In fact, I think things are getting worse instead of better. I see Chad's car at Peggy's place every afternoon and evening. I think she's isolating herself from us, Jen."

Jennifer nodded. "Binky said the same thing. Peggy's so wrapped up in Chad that she hasn't got time for any of her other friends anymore."

"Well," Lexi sighed, "I'm still her friend and I'm here if she needs me, but right now, Peggy's convinced she doesn't need us very much." It hurt to see one of her earliest friends in Cedar River acting this way. She and Peggy had so much in common from the very start. Now the gang—Todd, Jennifer, Binky, Egg and herself—seemed not quite whole without Peggy in their midst. Still, Lexi told herself, Chad was a nice boy and a handsome one. She could see why Peggy wanted to spend time with him.

"Well," she announced to Jennifer, her voice full of resolve she didn't feel, "I'm just not going to worry about it. I was honest with Peggy. I told her what I thought. If she can't accept that, then it's her problem, not mine. I miss her and if she knocked on our door this minute, I'd be the first one to welcome her in."

Jennifer nodded with understanding. "I know what you mean, but I have this gut feeling that we've lost Peggy, Lexi. She's not one of us anymore."

———

Not one of us anymore. It seemed as if Matt Windsor was having the same kind of trouble. The dark-jacketed boys who had tormented Ben seemed to have drifted away. Lexi no longer saw them around the school yard waiting for Matt after the final bell, but he had not replaced one group of friends with another. There was still a consensus around school that Matt Windsor was bad news, trouble, and someone to watch out for.

She and Todd, the only two who really knew what was going on in Matt's life, attempted to fill in the gap; but even they received pressure from Egg and Binky, who couldn't understand their sudden friendship with the wild boy. Until Matt himself was ready to explain, Todd and Lexi felt all they could do was to be there for him when he needed them.

Minda, on the other hand, had started a campaign to shame Matt back into being what he once was—her symbol of rebellion. That campaign became public in the next issue of the Cedar River High School paper.

Lexi and Todd were on their way out of school when Todd snapped his fingers. "Just a minute, Lexi. I want to pick up a copy of the paper. I haven't looked at it put together yet."

He grabbed two off the stack of the pile near the doorway and handed one to Lexi, taking the other for himself. After flipping through the paper to check the photo layout, Todd opened it to the column section. He winced as he scanned Minda's contribution.

"Who's changed most at Cedar River High?" the column began. "Who's made everyone stand up and take notice when he turned from macho to wimp? I'm not naming any names," Minda went on to write, "but I'll give you a clue: he shed his black leather jacket for plastic and polyester. Is there another nerd among us? Please spare us."

"Ouch," he yelped.

Lexi glanced up from the front page to ask, "What's wrong?"

"Minda really managed to savage Matt in this issue," he muttered. "Why Mrs. Drummond lets her get away with it, I'll never know."

Lexi peered over Todd's shoulder and read the offending column.

"For one thing, Minda insists that her columns are all in 'good fun.' I don't think Mrs. Drummond has any idea how often Minda uses it to humiliate people she's upset with."

"Maybe, maybe not. But those are fighting words about going from black leather to plastic and polyester. It could mean only one person that we know."

"She's disappointed," Lexi analyzed. "Matt was her reverse knight in shining armor. Now that he's left all that behind him, Minda doesn't understand why, and she feels as if he's let her down."

Todd stared at Lexi for a long moment. "You really do have people figured out, don't you, Lexi?"

"Usually," Lexi laughed. "But having them figured out and being able to do something about it are two different things."

As they were leaving the school ground, Matt Windsor caught up with them. "Hey! Wait up," he yelled.

"Hi, Matt," Lexi greeted him, glad to see the smile on his face. Of course, he might not have read the school paper yet. Then Matt's next words told her that he had.

"I see Minda Hannaford blasted me in her column this time," he said casually.

Todd glanced at him. "Do you mind?"

Matt shrugged. "It's not fun. I figure everyone in school could figure who she's referring to, but I kinda expected it."

"Oh?" Lexi said curiously.

Matt grinned. "Minda's been chasing me so hard this fall that I've been feeling like a rabbit with a hunting dog on my trail. I have a hunch she's been trying to prove to somebody how wild and daring she could be. Whether it was for the Hi-Five or her parents, I don't know." He looked down at the pale plaid shirt and corduroy jeans he wore. "Now that I've turned into a pussy cat, I guess I'm a big disappointment to her."

Lexi chuckled. "We were just saying the same thing, Matt. Minda's always looking for ways to be noticed. You went and ruined one of her chances."

Matt's brow furrowed. "I feel pretty guilty about Minda actually."

Both Todd and Lexi turned a curious gaze on Matt. "Guilty? Why?"

"Mostly about that party at the Williamses' house. Minda would never have thought smoking a joint of marijuana was cool if she didn't know that I did it."

"You can't say that, Matt," Lexi protested. "There's a lot of that going on in school. You can't blame yourself."

"But in Minda's case, I do. She was trying so hard to impress me back then that I think she would have tried just about anything."

Matt did have things pretty well figured out, Lexi realized. It was nice to know Matt was going to be okay.

A car door slammed and the threesome heard a low, irate muttering coming from a side street where many of the students parked their cars. "Dumb ol' thing. Dumb car. What am I supposed to do now, I'd like to know."

All three glanced around the corner to see Minda standing in front of her father's Mercedes. She gave a swift, useless kick to the tire and then a small yelp. She was hopping around on one foot, clutching her ankle in her hand when she looked up to see the three of them staring at her curiously.

"What are you looking at?" she barked. "Can't you go gawk somewhere else?"

"Car trouble, Minda?" Todd asked cheerfully. "Need a little help?"

Immediately, her sour expression changed to one more hopeful. "Could you?"

It was amazing, Lexi marveled, the number of moods Minda had at her disposal and how she could

turn them on and off instantly. Lexi did notice, however, that all of Minda's attention was focused on
Todd. She and Matt could have been pebbles on the
street as far as Minda was concerned.

Todd was sniffing the air. "Smells to me like you
flooded it, Minda. Were you pumping on the gas?"

Minda's eyes grew wide and innocent. "Why,
daddy told me never to do that."

"I realize that, Minda, but was that what you
were doing?"

Her face fell, "Well, it was just taking such a long
time to start . . ."

"Well, then I'd just give it a rest. It should start
on its own in a few minutes; don't you think so,
Matt?" Todd turned to where Matt and Lexi were
standing.

Matt nodded.

Minda turned coolly toward him. "Are you sure,
Matt? I thought all your information was about motorcycles, not Mercedes."

Matt, rather than responding to the bait that
Minda flung to trap him into an argument, merely
said, "Oh, I know a little about a lot of things, Minda,
but not as much as I should about others."

"What's that supposed to mean?" Minda sneered,
her lip curling into an unattractive twist.

"I just think I should apologize to you. I feel as if
it was my fault that night over at Tressa's house
when you were smoking—"

"Oh, that."

"I figure you were just trying to make an impres-
sion on me," Matt admitted. "And I'm sorry. I'm sorry
you thought I was the kind of guy you had to do that
for."

Minda gave him a cool, disbelieving stare as Matt stumbled on.

"I just don't want you to keep on doing it—"

"Don't worry," Minda huffed in her typical response. "I'm not going to mess up my brain. Especially for a guy who hasn't even figured out his own."

Turning up her nose, Minda whirled around, her skirt swinging around her knees as she scrambled into the Mercedes and slammed the door. This time when she turned the key, it jumped into life. Without a backward glance, she drove away, her head held high.

Minda was almost out of sight before the three of them burst out laughing. "Boy, did she ever put me in my place!" Matt finally managed to say when his chuckles had subsided.

"She certainly did," Lexi giggled.

"And you probably deserved every bit of it," Todd added.

Matt's smile faded a little. "I probably did. I guess I should have known better than to worry about Minda. She knows how to take care of herself better than anyone else I know. I guess I was the only really dumb one in the crowd."

Lexi remained silent, thinking about Matt's statement. Did Minda really know how to take care of herself? Minda had street smarts, that was true enough, and she could hold her own in an argument; but she suspected that deep down Minda wasn't much different from Matt. She was just as scared to show her pain as he had been.

Matt pulled on her sleeve, "Why so serious, Lexi?" He pointed to the front of his shirt. "Look, no blood. Minda didn't wound me at all."

"You're very lucky, you know. Most people who do battle with Minda come out scarred for life."

Matt smiled widely. "Lexi, you and Todd have shown me a way to get rid of the scars I've had all my life. You've shown me more about what life can and should be than I've ever realized was possible. Minda can throw all the sticks and stones and sharp words she wants, but it won't bother me because I've learned to give my hurt to God."

Lexi marveled at the placid expression on Matt's face. Could this be the same boy who had frightened her so with his dark, evil presence? What marvelous things can happen when God takes charge!

Chapter Thirteen

"More ice cream?"

"No way! No more ice cream, no more fudge sauce, no more peanuts, no more cake, no more anything!"

"Do you think they're full?" Jennifer inquired of Lexi, "Or are they just embarrassed to ask for sixths?"

Lexi giggled and glanced at Todd, Matt, and Egg sprawled across the Goldens' living room floor. Todd and Matt looked merely full, but Egg appeared slightly green.

"Best birthday I've had in years," Matt groaned. "If I live till tomorrow, I'm going to remember it with great pleasure."

"Very funny. No one sat on your chest and spooned food down your throat."

"Hah! I saw you sneak by my plate and dump another scoop of ice cream on it when you thought I wasn't looking!"

"It was an accident. It just slipped off my spoon."

"Right. You only had to shake it three times to get it to slip."

"Listen here, Matt Windsor. Are you calling me a liar? If you are . . ."

Binky and Lexi exchanged an amused glance. Jennifer and Matt had been at this all afternoon. Jennifer had finally found someone with a sense of humor like her own. Her renewed friendship with Matt had every sign of being a good one. And, of course, their little group—unlike that of Hi-Five's—had flexible, expandable walls. Everyone was more than happy to include Matt. Even Egg had come around now that Minda had given up her pursuit of him.

"Really, guys. This is great. Thanks." He looked at the few crumbs that were left of his birthday cake and then around the room. "I was worried about today, and look how it turned out. Thanks."

"How are things going at home?" Todd asked.

Matt shrugged. "They don't believe that I'm trying to change. Not yet, anyway. My stepmother still gets a worried look every time I walk into the room."

Jennifer put down the plate she was carrying and settled onto the floor crossing her legs Indian fashion. "You've got to have a little patience with them." She gave a wry smile. "Before I was diagnosed as a dyslexic, my parents couldn't believe what was happening to me either. Even now, I think my mom worries that I'll flip out and do something strange like dye my hair blue or pierce my nose. I know what you're going through."

It was amazing, Lexi mused, how God could take care of things that looked so hopeless and turn them into something good. Matt was like a new person these days.

He'd taken over as a helper in the lower levels of Sunday school at church. He could manage the children far better than the former helper, and at the same time he could hear the Gospel just as a little child would hear it.

Lexi hadn't appreciated that fact until one day Matt had pointed out to her the verse in Proverbs 22:6: "Train up a child in the way he should go, and when he is old, he will not depart from it." Then he found the verse in Matthew 18:3 that said, "Except ye be converted, and become as little children, ye shall not enter into the kingdom of heaven."

"It's my chance, Lexi," he'd told her, "to hear everything from a child's perspective. To see how they accept things without questioning and how willing they are to believe." He'd given her a glimpse of an impish smile. "I'm pretty cynical about things. I need to see the children's absolute, unquestioning faith. Can you understand that?"

The more Lexi considered it, the more sense it made. It was Matt's way of finding himself, his way of using his bright, questioning mind to develop a concrete faith. Matt would find his way. Lexi was sure of it.

"Whatcha thinking about, Lexi?" Binky inquired. "You look so serious." Then her attention shifted to her brother Egg. "I know better than to ask what Egg is thinking about. It's always the same thing. Minda."

Egg flushed a hot pink.

"Well, you *were*, weren't you?"

The blush turned scarlet.

"Told you so."

Jennifer, who'd gone to the kitchen for a moment,

entered the room innocent of the brief conversation
between brother and sister to announce, "Know what
I heard yesterday? Minda Hannaford has found a
new love interest! You know that new student
teacher in the typing department? The one with the
black curly hair?" She nodded sagely. "Well, that's
the one. Poor guy doesn't even know what's coming!"

Lexi had seen beets from her mother's garden
that were paler than Egg's face.

Egg swallowed twice as if to recover his compo-
sure. Then a wobbly, tentative smile tilted his lips.

"It's okay, you guys. Don't look so horrified. I
know all about Minda." He rubbed his hands together. "I understand her and I like her anyway."
His head drooped forward and a stray lock of hair
tumbled across his forehead. "I know. I'm crazy, but
hey!" he said, looking up and spreading his hands
wide, "it's a free country! I can be crazy if I want to!"

Todd and Matt burst out laughing and Lexi
clapped her hands.

"That's the spirit, Egg-O, my man!"

"Don't let anyone get you down!"

Egg blushed again. "By the way, Matt," he began,
"since you aren't wearing that black leather jacket
anymore, I was wondering if you'd let me borrow it?
Just for a few days? See, I can rent this bike and ride
it to school and I thought if Minda saw me she
might . . ."

Laughing, Lexi picked up some of the clutter of
dirty dishes and carried them to the kitchen. She was
standing over the sink gazing out the window when
she felt someone come up behind her.

It was Matt. Silently he moved to stand beside
her and together they looked out into the gathering
dusk.

"It isn't easy, is it?" Lexi murmured.

"What?"

"Life. Look at what's going on. Peggy and Chad. Egg and his hopeless crush on Minda . . ."

"Me."

Lexi turned to stare at him.

"You know," he began, "for a while I thought things would be easier for me. I thought that as soon as I changed my clothes and quit hanging out with a bad bunch, that my dad and my teachers would trust me again. I even thought that somehow my mom would get word how things had changed and she'd come back."

"And?"

"And it's not easier at all. Now, no one can figure me out. They talk about how I've changed, but they don't believe it's for real."

Lexi felt Matt shudder. "Sometimes I think things might even be worse. At least when I used my tough guy act I didn't feel so . . . vulnerable." He gave a sad smile. "I guess drugs and black leather can make you feel powerful."

Lexi leaned forward and put her elbows on the rim of the sink, cupping her chin in her hands. "But you've got access to more power now, Matt. The biggest source of power in the universe."

"I'm beginning to realize that, Lexi, but it takes time. There's still so much I don't understand about God or His Son."

"You will. Just don't give up. Don't get disappointed because you expected your life to change all of a sudden and it hasn't."

Matt gave a long leisurely stretch. His face was

more relaxed and composed than Lexi had ever remembered seeing it.

"This way isn't easier, just better. My new life is
as much of a struggle as the old one." Then he cocked
his head and indicated that they should return to the
living room where a very noisy discussion had broken out. "But, you know, Lexi, this is one battle I
plan to win."

———

Matt may have won his battle, but what do Peggy
and Chad have to face? Can Peggy and Lexi's friendship withstand the predicament Peggy finds herself
in? Find out in Cedar River Daydreams #5.

A Note From Judy

I'm glad you're reading *Cedar River Daydreams*! I hope I've given you something to think about as well as a story to entertain you. If you feel you have any of the problems that Lexi and her friends experience, I encourage you to talk with your parents, a pastor, or a trusted adult friend. There are many people who care about you!

Also, I enjoy hearing from my readers, so if you'd like to write, my address is:

Judy Baer
Bethany House Publishers
6820 Auto Club Road
Minneapolis, MN 55438

Please include an addressed, stamped envelope if you would like an answer. Thanks.